KB

A Candlelight Ecstasy Romance®

"JUST HOW MANY STRINGS DID YOU PULL TO GET THIS JOB FOR ME?" JEFF DEMANDED.

"Your firm was highly recommended and I didn't ask for any opinions," Paige answered.

"Ah, a royal edict." Jeff exhaled slowly. "Do you think it was worth the risk?"

"It is, Jeff. I don't know what happened to the specification sheets, but I know you didn't take them and—"

"Such blind faith in my integrity." He sounded crisp and cynical. "A little late, Paige, just a bit too late."

"If that were true, you wouldn't be here. You believe there's a chance to find out what really happened two years ago and together we can—"

"Oh, no, there's no 'together we can,' Paige. I needed your help then. I don't need it now."

CANDLELIGHT ECSTASY ROMANCES®

394 LOVER AND DECEIVER, *Cathie Linz*
395 THE CAPE COD AFFAIR, *Edith Delatush*
396 PASSION'S ROGUE, *Helen Carras*
397 WRITTEN IN THE STARS, *Linda Randall Wisdom*
398 THE GAMBLER'S GAME, *Lee Magner*
399 AT LONG LAST LOVE, *Andrea St. John*
400 JEWELED SKIES, SHIMMERING SANDS, *Anna Hudson*
401 LINGERING LAUGHTER, *JoAnna Brandon*
402 HEIGHTS OF DESIRE, *Molly Katz*
403 MORE THAN SKIN DEEP, *Emily Elliott*
404 A MOMENT'S ENCHANTMENT, *Jane Atkin*
405 SEDUCED BY A STRANGER, *Barbara Andrews*
406 A LOVE OF OUR OWN, *Lori Copeland*
407 SHEER DELIGHT, *Cory Kenyon*
408 MYSTERY LADY, *Eleanor Woods*
409 TOGETHER IN THE NIGHT, *Candace McCarthy*
410 SWEET-TIME LOVIN', *Blair Cameron*
411 SING SOFTLY TO ME, *Dorothy Phillips*
412 ALL A MAN COULD WANT, *Linda Randall Wisdom*
413 SOMETHING WILD AND FREE, *Helen Conrad*
414 TO THE HIGHEST BIDDER, *Neva Beach*
415 HANDS OFF THE LADY, *Elise Randolph*
416 WITH EVERY KISS, *Sheila Paulos*
417 DREAM MAKER, *Donna Kimel Vitek*

A WOMAN'S TOUCH

Karen Whittenburg

A CANDLELIGHT ECSTASY ROMANCE®

Published by
Dell Publishing Co., Inc.
1 Dag Hammarskjold Plaza
New York, New York 10017

ISBN: 0-440-10513-7

Printed in the United States of America

April 1986

10 9 8 7 6 5 4 3 2 1

WFH

To Lydia,
who gave me the opportunity,
the encouragement,
and the confidence.
Thank-you doesn't begin to express my
gratitude.

To Our Readers:

We have been delighted with your enthusiastic response to Candlelight Ecstasy Romances®, and we thank you for the interest you have shown in this exciting series.

In the upcoming months we will continue to present the distinctive, sensuous love stories you have come to expect only from Ecstasy. We look forward to bringing you many more books from your favorite authors and also the very finest work from new authors of contemporary romantic fiction.

As always, we are striving to present the unique, absorbing love stories that you enjoy most—books that are more than ordinary romance. Your suggestions and comments are always welcome. Please write to us at the address below.

Sincerely,

The Editors
Candlelight Romances
1 Dag Hammarskjold Plaza
New York, New York 10017

CHAPTER ONE

Silence dominated the boardroom for a moment before the throat clearing and skeptical chuckles began and then, just as abruptly, died. Only one of the six men present looked at her, leaving five to shift uncomfortably in the cushioned leather chairs. Paige was oddly pleased by the shock value of her announcement. If there hadn't been so much at stake, she would have smiled. Instead, she met Edward's disapproval with a steady regard.

"Paige," he said slowly in a voice soft with paternal authority, "we cannot offer the job to Jefferson Lawrence."

How like her stepfather to pronounce Jeff's name as if it were merely a filled-in blank on an application form! Paige lowered her eyes to the hands she clasped loosely on the tabletop and steeled herself to subvert the opposition.

"It's taken a long time and a great deal of effort to secure this contract with Tri-Star and we have our best technicians ready to begin work on it. It's unfortunate that Jacob's heart condition is forcing him to retire, but it could be disastrous for Randall Electronics if we don't hire someone to replace him immediately. Hiring a consulting firm is the quickest, most practical option open to us and Lawrence Associates comes highly recommended."

She kept her tone firm, reasonable, and calm, even though her body ached with tension. "I'm sure all of you will agree that Jeff is the most qualified engineer we could hope to find and he knows this company inside and out."

"That's one way of putting it, I suppose."

Paige turned a cool stare to the man who had spoken. Mitchell Brewer was annoying under any circumstances, but now his snide demeanor grated against her control. "If you have an objection, Mitch, say so. We don't have time for pointless remarks."

"All right," Mitch said, his tone as brash as the impudent challenge in his pale blue eyes. "Why should we offer Lawrence a chance to steal from the company again?"

"Again?" It was hard to keep her voice low and steady, but necessary. Very necessary. "Do you know something the rest of us don't, Mitch?"

The corner of his mouth twitched and tightened. "Lack of evidence is not proof of innocence."

"Or guilt."

"He's a lousy risk, Paige. You, of all people, should know that."

Her knuckles went white as the room became oppressively close and stifling. She was aware of the glances the other board members turned first to her, then to Mitch, and finally to Edward, who coughed, a muffled, distracted sort of sound, yet when he spoke he had control of the meeting once again. "Paige. Mitchell. Let's keep the discussion relevant."

"Dammit! This is relevant." Mitch slapped the walnut tabletop with his palm. "Evidence or no, Jeff Lawrence stole the specs for the NaeComp contract and sold them to the highest bidder. In the aftermath, we lost two sizable contracts and who knows how many others. I've spent the past twenty-four months assuring computer firms across the nation that Randall Electronics has plugged the leak, that it can't happen again. Why should I sit here and let her"—he indicated Paige with a jerk of his blond head—"sacrifice the company just because she's having second thoughts about her divorce?"

Edward Glendenning rose, his height only slightly less imposing than his authoritative manner. "Mitchell, as the *owner,* Paige naturally cares about the firm and you know as well as I do she would never allow her private life to influence her decisions on company matters." He smiled a dismissal. "Let's adjourn for today and continue this discussion tomorrow."

"No." Paige's objection was lost in the shuffle of chairs being thrust back and the low drone of conversation as the board members prepared to leave the room. "No," she repeated loudly, stopping all movement and bringing every gaze to her face. She remained seated, facing the men with a resolve born of desperation. "I want Jeff to be the project manager on this contract. There's no reason to discuss it further."

"Well, I'll be—" Mitch's protest was cut short.

"Thank you, gentlemen," Edward interrupted the discontented rumblings and, with a curt nod, discouraged further comment. Five men filed silently from the room. Paige watched them go, knowing she had merely fired the opening shot. Her stepfather wouldn't be easily persuaded. And in this case he had the tactical advantage.

She followed his movements with her eyes as he closed the door and returned to his chair at the opposite end of the table. He was tall and spare, a distinguished-looking man, with hair only a shade away from silver. It had been a rich deep brown when Paige had first met him. Sixteen years had passed since her mother had introduced an awkward, preadolescent Paige to her soon-to-be stepfather. She had been apprehensive then; she was no less apprehensive now.

He closed the leather-bound notebook he always brought with him into the boardroom and slowly turned his attention to her. A corner of his mouth lifted in ambiguous parental understanding. Paige waited.

"You might, at least, have given me some advance warning, Paige. We could have discussed your—preference in consulting firms before the meeting and avoided the scene with Brewer."

"It isn't simply a preference. I want you to offer the position to Jeff." She moistened her lips. "I didn't tell you before because I knew you'd try to change my mind. You can't, Edward. No one can."

His thin lips softened to placate her. "Can we talk about it now? Is that against the rules?"

There were no rules this time, she thought, no standard manual of professional ethics to follow. There was just a wrong that needed to be righted. And hope. Ever that elusive hope. "I suppose we must talk about it. Mitch only said what a lot of people will think."

"With good cause."

Her chin snapped up. "Jeff didn't steal those papers."

Edward tapped his finger against the embossed symbol on the notebook cover. "Paige, you can't make up to Jeff for what happened. I don't think he'd accept the position anyway. Why would he want to come back when it would mean opening up the whole scandal again? I doubt he will even consider taking a job with us."

She could think of only one reason and she wasn't optimistic about it. "He deserves the satisfaction of refusing. We owe him that much, Edward."

"Jeff made his own choices. No one asked him to resign."

"No one asked him to stay, either." Nor had she. Could she ever make him understand? Would he even give her a chance to try? Paige toyed with one of the tiny pearl buttons at her cuff. "Edward, we were wrong to let him leave like that. We should never have agreed to stop the investigation, no matter what the consequences to the company."

"It was what Jeff wanted," Edward said irritably. "My God, Paige, don't you remember how adamant he was?"

She didn't. Her memories of that afternoon were indistinct, like out-of-focus photographs that no amount of regret could clarify. She only remembered the way Jeff had avoided looking at her . . . and the nauseating confusion of her own uncertainty. "It doesn't matter, Edward. The fact remains, we let Jeff leave under a cloud of suspicion and instead of getting to the bottom of the theft, we swept it under the rug, cut our losses, and went on with business as though nothing had happened."

Edward stroked his angular chin, as if the neatly clipped beard he'd once worn were still in place. Then he left his end of the table to take the chair beside Paige. "It's a little late for regrets," he said. "Both professional and personal. Something *did* happen, Paige. The papers were stolen and the evidence did implicate Jeff. *He* chose not to explain why he was in the building that night or why he had cleared out his office. It wasn't your choice and it wasn't mine, so I really don't see what more we could have done."

Logically, of course, he was right. But over the course of two lonely years, she had come to understand that logic sometimes made no sense whatsoever. "I want to do something now. Maybe it is too little, too late, but I want to make the gesture. I hope you'll understand, but if not. . . ." She left the sentence hanging, reluctant to complete the threat, yet unwilling to back down. "If push comes to shove and it goes to a vote, Mother will support me on this. You know she will, Edward."

His smile curved in rueful acknowledgment. "She spoils you, Paige, but then I suppose the same could be said of me. I wouldn't be much of a parent, though, if I didn't try to discourage you this time. Offering the Tri-Star project to Jeff is not in the company's best interest. And it isn't in your best interest, either. The divorce has been final for well over a year now and you haven't heard a single word from Jeff in all that time." Edward reached to pat her hand. "Your mother and I have talked about this, Paige, and frankly, we're concerned about you. Haven't you mourned your marriage long enough?"

With a soft sigh, she rose and walked to the window. "I don't expect you—I don't expect anyone—to understand. This is something I have to do."

"Do you think the offer of this consulting job will bring Jeff back to you? Do you want a reconciliation, Paige? Is that the reason behind all this? Is that why you've officially kept Paige Lawrence as your name instead of changing it back to Randall?"

A reconciliation was hardly within the realm of possibility. "My reasons are my own. Please don't ask me to explain or defend them, Edward."

"That's a pretty tall order, dear."

Her smile went wry with affection. "Speaking as company president or as my stepfather?"

"Both." He stood, but made no move to cross the room and the hard-won boundaries of her independence. "I think you're making a mistake. There's no doubt that Jeff is the most qualified man in the area for this particular contract, but if he should actually accept the job . . ."

Paige turned from the silent warning and looked through the window to the buildings that housed Randall Electronics . . . *her* company, jointly owned with her mother, founded by her father years before when the computer age was only a hypothesis. Was she risking its future for the expiation of a nebulous guilt? Or was she simply weighing one loyalty against another and finding the scales out of balance? Restlessly, she pressed a palm to the cool glass. "How soon will you get in touch with him, Edward?"

There was a sharp, deliberate pause, and though she wasn't watching, Paige knew he was frowning. "I'll write a letter this afternoon," Edward said in a voice that revealed none of the reservations she knew he harbored, but let her know he disapproved nonetheless. "Jeff should receive it first thing Monday morning."

"Thank you." She turned to face her stepfather, wishing there were something more meaningful she could say. "I hope you understand, Edward, that this has nothing to do with you. You've always done a wonderful job in managing the company, watching after Mother's interests . . . and mine. You know I have no designs on your job and I'd never pull rank on you like this if it wasn't—" She broke off, not knowing exactly how to complete the thought. Was this gesture of good faith really necessary? Or was she simply justifying the means to an end? "This is very . . . important to me."

"I know, Paige, but . . ." He paused, then resolutely picked up his notebook and walked to the door. "Well, we'll just have to see what happens. In all probability, Jeff won't read past the letterhead."

"You could be right."

"I hope I am, Paige. For a lot of reasons, I sincerely hope that I am." With a wistful sort of smile, Edward stepped into the hallway, closing the door behind him and leaving her alone in the boardroom. Paige turned back to the window and, with a thumb and forefinger, massaged the bridge of her nose.

It was done, she thought, the first step taken. Now, if only Jeff would meet her halfway . . .

The buzz of the telephone was an irritation. So was the distant clatter of a typewriter beyond his office door. Jeff tossed his pen to the desk and reached for the button on the intercom.

"Hold my calls." He clipped the words at the box and the secretary on the other end. He didn't wait for a response before he pushed back his chair and rose to pace the length of the room. Realizing the futility of his annoyance, he sank onto the cushions of the leather sofa and loosened the knot of his tie.

It was a nice office, he thought with a glance around, comfortable, convenient, and a definite improvement over the cubicle he'd called his own at Randall Electronics. He had a nice life now too. Perhaps it wasn't a tremendous improvement over his life before, but at least he felt in control. So why had a single letter thrown his perspective out of kilter?

Paige. She was responsible for the letter and for his irritability. Edward's signature might be on the paper, but Paige's manipulative finger had guided the pen. Under the circumstances, Jeff couldn't quite pinpoint her motives, but he was sure they lay somewhere between the lines of Glendenning's crisp, concise job offer.

It sounded forthright enough, Jeff thought. Randall Electronics had contracted to build a microchip, which in turn would be used by Tri-Star to fulfill their contract with the United States government. He'd consulted with other computer manufacturers on similar contracts and he was familiar with both companies involved. Still, this was a little more than a basic consultation: Paige wanted him to be project manager and oversee the production. Whatever else she might have in mind, he had no desire to discover. It was a moot point, anyway. Going back was not his style. Still . . .

He couldn't deny that he was tempted. He'd thought he'd come to grips with all that had happened, that he'd pulled himself past the point of wanting to vindicate his innocence. But now a couple of typewritten paragraphs had brought it all back—the anger, the betrayal, the helplessness, everything. And, again, Paige was responsible.

A brusque knock on the door was followed by Toby's wide grin and lanky frame. "So," he said, "this is what you do when you don't answer the intercom. It's early in the week for apathy on the job, Lawrence. This is Monday, remember?"

Jeff lifted one corner of his mouth in halfhearted greeting. "So it is."

"I can see you're not in the mood to discuss computer malfunctions."

"That obvious, huh?" Jeff leaned against the sofa back and crossed an ankle at his knee. "Actually, I'm contemplating a job offer."

"Apparently not with much enthusiasm." Toby's eyebrows rose with mercenary interest. "How good an offer is it?"

"I haven't decided."

"If the company is solvent, it's a good offer. We haven't been in the consulting business long enough to turn away paying customers."

"Salary isn't important in this case. There are other . . . factors."

Toby settled onto the corner of the desk, crossed his arms, and assumed an indulgent expression. "Get serious, Jeff. You can have as many 'factors' as you want, but just between us, money is the only one that counts."

"Not this time." Jeff waved a hand toward the desk top. "Take a look at that letter."

Toby obliged, his forehead wrinkling all the way to his receding hairline as he scanned the sheet of paper. Lifting his head, he gave a low whistle. "Randall Electronics. Now, isn't that a kick? Just when you're getting the hang of roller skating, someone sticks out a foot and tries to trip you up."

"Not someone, my ex-wife." The word tasted bitter in his mouth and Jeff realized it was the first time he'd referred to Paige in that way. There should have been a certain satisfaction in verbally relegating her to the past. But he felt only an aching emptiness. "Paige," he clarified, although Toby had heard her name dozens of times before, "is behind this. Edward Glendenning would never have offered this job to our firm if she hadn't insisted. I just can't imagine why she would."

"Oh, come on, Jeff. You were married—what? Three years? You must have some idea."

Absently, Jeff began to tap his fingers against his leg. "I suppose she might be trying to soothe a guilty conscience."

"Or . . . ?"

He didn't want to think about the other possibilities. "How the hell should I know? I could never explain why she did the things she did when we were married. It would be foolish to try to analyze her motives now."

"Well, don't let that stop you. It's been a long time since you did anything foolish."

"It's been exactly fourteen and a half minutes. I shouldn't have opened that envelope. A little curiosity can be deadly."

Toby pursed his mouth in friendly dispute. "Live dangerously. Accept the position and see what develops."

"I know what will develop—a king-sized headache."

"And maybe the answers to some very important questions."

Jeff sighed and rubbed the tension in his shoulder muscles. "*I* know I didn't steal those spec sheets, Toby. It doesn't matter what anyone else thinks."

The silence was more eloquent than any argument could have been. Jeff knew, just as Toby knew, that it did matter. For almost two years, he'd allowed peripheral issues to cloud his perspective. It was time and past to take a long, steady look at *his* motives. "But I'm going to give this 'golden' opportunity serious consideration just the same."

Toby nodded a benign approval as he stood and brushed the wrinkles from his trouser legs. "Let's go to lunch."

"Now?" Jeff glanced at his watch—a first-anniversary gift from Paige. He didn't know why he still wore it.

"Too early?" Toby asked. "All right, you're the senior partner. I'll come back in an hour."

"For someone who's worried about the checking account, you don't seem too concerned about doing any work."

"Have it your way. I'll be back in two hours." Which would still be only eleven-thirty, but Toby didn't linger to argue. "We can talk about that computer malfunction then."

Alone again, Jeff stared at the carpet, thinking—not for the first time—that Paige's eyes were the same gray-blue shade. He should have chosen a different color for his office. With a sigh, he pushed to his feet and walked to the desk. The letter lay where Toby had dropped it and Jeff frowned with a nagging disquiet.

Edward certainly hadn't made any effort to personalize the letter. It was written on company stationery according to company policy. There was nothing that hinted of the once-close working relationship between the writer of the letter and the recipient. There was nothing, in fact, to indicate Jefferson Lawrence had had any prior connection with Randall Electronics.

Unfortunately, memory provided all the connection necessary. From his first nervous interview for a part-time job to the day he'd finished college and stepped into his own private office, through each promotion and every achievement, he could reminisce at will. He remembered the day Charles Randall had died. And he remembered the day Edward Glendenning had become company president. Oddly, he didn't remember his first introduction to Paige. It had slipped past, unnoticed, until later.

Before he realized what he was doing, the letter lay crumpled in his fist. *Paige.* No matter which way he turned, she was there. It should have stopped hurting. The regrets should have faded. He should have grown indifferent.

And he certainly shouldn't give serious consideration to accepting the position with Randall Electronics. Saying he intended to do so had seemed a good way to twist the conversation with Toby into a less personal vein. Toby knew the circumstances under which Jeff had left the company, but he didn't know the part Paige had played in the disillusionment. There were times, weak moments, when Jeff wondered if Paige realized her contribution to the irreconcilable differences that had ended their marriage.

Maybe she had. Maybe that had prompted the job offer. The thought made him uncomfortably aware of emotions he'd tried hard to forget. What did she want? And if he went back, could he be objective?

Jeff sat on the corner of his desk, pleating his doubts into the wadded paper in his hand. *If* he went back, it would be for one reason—to find out who had stolen the NaeComp spec sheets and why. It might be too late. Two years was a long time. But then so was a lifetime of regret, and this opportunity wouldn't come again. In all probability, he would eventually have decided to return to Tulsa and the unanswered questions on his own. Paige simply had offered both the opportunity and a legitimate cover for his presence within the company. Deliberately? Did she hope he could prove his innocence?

An old injustice stirred his anger. He would prove it. But not for her. He owed this to himself. At first he had just wanted to get away, to put as much distance as possible between himself and Paige. The mileage between Oklahoma City and Tulsa wasn't that great, but it had proved to be far enough. He only hoped it would remain so.

Going back would place him in a vulnerable position. Everyone would be watching him, taking note of his actions and wondering, always wondering. But that was all right. He'd be doing a lot of watching and wondering himself.

Paige, though, was the unknown factor, the risk he couldn't define. She was a part of all he wanted to forget and of all he had to remember.

With sudden decision, he smoothed out Edward's letter and reached for the intercom switch. "Let's go to lunch," he said when Toby answered. "There are some things I want to talk over with you."

"What? Now?"

Jeff chuckled, feeling oddly lighthearted. "Of course, now. There's no time like the present. Haven't you heard?"

CHAPTER TWO

"It's my pleasure to present this engraved plaque to the Business and Professional Men's Man of the Year —Edward R. Glendenning!"

Paige joined the applause and shared a proud smile with her mother across the room. Mary Glendenning added a touch of springtime to the somber white and silver decor of the head table. In lavender blue, with a broad-brimmed hat that no other woman in the room could have worn with such style, she was an intangible cut above the rest. As a child, Paige had wanted to be a carbon copy—blond hair, green eyes, that cool aura of mystery. But capricious fate had dictated differently and Paige, like her father, was dark-haired, blue-eyed, and hardly ever mysterious.

Jeff hadn't seemed to mind, she remembered. He'd told her time and again that all gentlemen did not prefer blondes. In fact, Jeff had thought she was pretty near perfect . . . once. Paige sighed. Why couldn't she forget all the things he'd *once* said to her or thought about her? It seemed so futile to remember.

As Mary's smile turned to Edward, who now stood at the podium accepting his plaque, Paige's thoughts turned with distracted curiosity to the people around her. Practically every person she knew was in the banquet room of the Westin Hotel. Certainly, every person who held a place in her heart was present, except one.

Her eyes scanned the tables, looking for Jeff as she always seemed to be looking for him. He wasn't there. She'd verified his absence with a visual check upon first entering the room. Not that she'd expected him to come. He'd been in Tulsa a full week, and in that time she hadn't caught a single glimpse of him. Even the one morning he'd been at the plant, Jeff had managed to avoid her. Or perhaps he'd simply managed to forget her.

This isn't going to work, she thought. The idea of bringing Jeff back within talking distance had been an outside shot at best. She'd known that all along, but already she was too emotionally involved, too hopeful. The odds weren't on her side. A gambler would bet against her. With a frown, Paige reached for her water and sipped. Whom was she kidding? The world's greatest chump would bet against her.

Edward's words of acceptance were said and Paige joined the applause again as he resumed his seat at the head table. In a matter of minutes, the reception was over and the crowd began its slow progress toward the exit. Paige stood, pushed in her chair, and said a preliminary good-bye to the friends who had shared her table. Glancing at the group of well-wishers surrounding her mother and Edward, Paige decided to wait for them to join her.

"Hey, sweetheart, let's slip out the back and find a place with some action."

She turned to look up at Mitchell Brewer, speculating on just how much action he had in mind. Not that it required a vivid imagination. "You slip out the back, Mitch. I'll take my chances here."

His hand went to her shoulder and stayed there as his lips rolled into a practiced smile. "You're wasting your time."

She stood, moving her shoulder out of reach with a careless shrug. "Ah, well, live and learn."

"I keep trying, but . . ." Mitch glanced past her and finished the thought with a raised eyebrow. "Now I'm beginning to get the picture. And my opinion stays the same—you are definitely wasting your time."

Paige tightened her lips in annoyance. "Then don't let me take up any more of yours."

"Hello, Brewer." The voice was Jeff's. Behind her, just to the left. Everything froze—the noisy hum of conversation, the restless movements of a crowd too long confined, the clatter of dishes, and the bustle of the restaurant cleaning crew. It all stopped. The only sound she could hear was her thundering heartbeat, the only movement was her slow-motion pirouette.

It couldn't be Jeff. Not now. She'd wanted time to think, a moment to know he was near before facing his perceptive brown eyes. But there wasn't time. He was here. Now. And her throat closed with emotion as she stared up at him. He was still tall. An inane observation, she thought, but somehow endearing. Just reminiscing on the times they'd endured "Mutt and Jeff" remarks began a melting warmth in her stomach.

"Hello, Jeff." Her greeting was no more than a whisper. He wasn't even looking at her. He was watching Mitch, listening to the subtle hostility in the other man's voice, bracing himself for either an insincere handshake or a right hook to his left jaw. But despite that, he heard her soft hello and was aware—in all his most vulnerable places—of a stirring emotion. He glanced in her direction and looked quickly away, not allowing his eyes to linger, not permitting himself to fully appreciate the special combination of beauty and charm that was uniquely Paige's.

Mitchell Brewer was apparently still deciding whether or not he should shake the hand Jeff offered. But it wasn't an open-ended invitation and Jeff brought his hand back to his side, belatedly realizing he ought to acknowledge Paige. "Hello, Paige," he said with a bare nod of his head. "How are you?"

How are you? They had been married, desperately in love, and after two years of separation he said, *how are you,* as if there had been nothing between them. Nothing. But then what had she expected? Their marriage had dissolved in anger, their love had melted with the heat of too many disagreements.

Maybe she simply should be grateful that he'd spoken to her at all. Paige stared at his handsome features—the toasty gold hair, the dark-lashed brown eyes, the strong, stubborn jaw—she knew him so well. Yet she knew so little about him.

"I'm fine," she said, but the words were lost in Mitch's swaggering drawl.

"I've been out of the office, but I'd heard you were back, Lawrence. Not that I believe every *rumor* I hear, you understand."

The air fairly bristled with antagonism, but Jeff didn't allow his composure to falter. "That's good to know, Brewer. Shows what a discriminating listener you are."

Mitch's response was just as cool, just as wary. "Oh, absolutely. I keep my eyes and ears open at all times."

"Not to mention your mouth." Paige took a verbal step into the ring and dared Mitch to take a swing at her. "Excuse us, please. I know Jeff will want to say hello to Mother and Edward."

"Oh, of course. This is, after all, a 'family affair,' isn't it, Paige?"

She would have planted a heel full-square on his instep if Jeff hadn't grabbed her arm and steered her away. "Forget it, Paige," he said in an undertone. "Brewer isn't worth it."

"No." It was not an agreement, but a protest against the wave of sensation spreading through her. It was just a touch—his hand on her arm. There was even a silky sleeve of material in between, but she was beginning to tremble with the contact. This wasn't the reaction she had planned. Calm, composed, that's what she'd intended to be. Not this nervous, tip-to-toe tingle of excitement and apprehension.

"I see he still has 'plans' for you," Jeff continued as he maneuvered around cloth-draped tables and the few remaining groups of the dwindling crowd. "He doesn't discourage easily, does he?"

Paige slipped free of his touch. "Maybe I don't try to discourage Mitch anymore. Maybe I have 'plans' for him."

"Like hell you do." Jeff moved ahead of her, then slowed his steps as a corner of his mouth lifted in wry apology. "We've had this discussion before, haven't we?"

"Many times." And she remembered each one. Some had been her fault, some had been his. But all had been angry clashes based on unfounded jealousy and the insecurity that had shadowed the last year of their marriage. "We couldn't seem to reach a satisfactory conclusion then either."

His grin came easily and held a reminiscent tenderness. "Oh, I wouldn't say that. As I recall, there were moments of deep satisfaction."

She dipped her chin in reluctance to share the memory and Jeff wished he hadn't mentioned it. He wished he didn't remember the passion that had flared from their anger to span the intangible distance between their hearts. But he couldn't forget. Even now, with so many bridges burned, he felt the low throb of desire and knew he wasn't completely past wanting her. Not quite. "Two years hasn't been all that long, has it?" he asked, hoping to bring her eyes back to him.

"I suppose time is a matter of perspective." Paige lifted her gaze to his with disquieting honesty. "It's been the longest two years of my life."

What could he say to that? He'd be damned if he'd apologize. He'd be damned if he knew what to apologize for. The divorce had been no-fault only in theory. She could have stopped it if she'd wanted. But then, he supposed, so could he. What did it matter? He turned, looking for a familiar face, a change of tension.

"Jefferson!" Mary came toward him with a smile, one hand extended. In a moment, he was being hugged as closely as her hat would allow. Maternal instincts died hard, he supposed, but at the moment he was glad that Mary cared more for him than for any legality.

"I couldn't believe my eyes when you came through those doors." Mary laughed as she stepped back and resettled the tilt of her hat. "Why did you hide in the back like that? There were plenty of places to sit." Pausing again, Mary beamed her approval. "You look wonderful. I've been worried that you weren't taking care of yourself. So many divorced men don't, you know." She shook her head. "It's so good to see you, Jeff."

Paige loved her mother all the more for welcoming Jeff as the son she'd always considered him. Yet deep in her heart, Paige resented the circumstances that left her on the outside of this affectionate reunion.

"You're looking as beautiful as ever, Mary." Jeff reverted to a charming deference to which Paige could never remember being treated. But then, he'd never had to try very hard to charm her.

"It *is* good to see you," Mary repeated. "Edward will be delighted that you came to the reception."

Edward, who joined them in a moment, didn't appear delighted. In accepting the position with Randall Electronics, Jeff had expected a certain amount of displeasure. He'd been prepared, in fact, to answer a lot of questions from his former in-law. After all, Edward was protective of his family and of the company. But in a week's time, there had been no questions, only a casual communication that allowed them to discuss the Tri-Star contract and other related business matters.

"Glad you could come" was Edward's only comment other than a "thank you" when Jeff congratulated him on winning the professional award. An older couple, bridge partners of the Glendennings, stopped to admire Edward's plaque and to suggest a nightcap in the hotel clubroom. Mary and Edward accepted and promised to join their friends in a few minutes. "Come with us," Mary urged Jeff when the other couple had left. "You, too, Paige. It will give us a chance to catch up on what Jeff's been doing."

"Mother." Paige made the protest under her breath. Didn't Mary realize she was creating an impossibly awkward situation? "I'm sure Jeff doesn't—"

"I'd like that. Thank you." Jeff avoided visual contact, knowing he would see irritation in Paige's eyes. She didn't want him included in the invitation, no matter how rude it might be to exclude him. That was why he'd accepted. To show Paige he was no longer affected by her wishes. But, of course, the very thought showed how affected he *still* was. Damn! Where was all the careful indifference he'd possessed before entering the banquet room—before seeing Paige again?

"It's been a long day. I think I'll just go home." Despite her best intentions, Paige glanced at Jeff as she made her excuses. *Home.* Did he ever think about all the times the two of them had gone home together? Hundreds of evenings when home had been theirs. Not just hers. Or his. "Good night, Mother, Edward." She paused, remembering, wondering if he was remembering too. "Good night . . . Jeff."

His throat closed around a knot of emotion. He couldn't explain it. There was no logical reason for him to feel anything. She'd only said good night. It was just a formality. It meant nothing. But the memories it brought . . .

"Be careful, darling." Mary tapped Paige on the cheek. "Lock the doors before you start the car. And check the back seat. You can't be too careful, you know. Even in an attended parking area."

"Mother—"

"I'll walk you to your car, Paige." Now why had he said that? Jeff would have liked to believe it was merely courtesy, but he knew better. He wanted to ensure her safety, protect her from imaginary fears as he had done in the past. It had been his responsibility, his privilege, then. It wasn't anymore.

Her eyes, more gray now than blue, assessed his motive with surprise and suspicion. "No," she said evenly. "It isn't necessary."

"But, Paige—"

Leaning forward, Paige stopped her mother's protest with a kiss on the cheek. "Have a good time, Mother." She moved to kiss her stepfather too. "I am proud of you, Edward." Purposely turning away from Jeff, Paige walked to the doorway, knowing his gaze followed, wondering if he felt even a shadow of the empty regrets that trailed her.

Balancing on one stockinged foot, Paige reached down to slip the remaining navy-blue pump from her heel. Lifting it absently, she looked around the room. The bedroom she had shared with Jeff. Once she'd thrown a shoe, very much like the one she now held, at him. There had been a small tear in the wallpaper for several months afterward. She had refused to apply the mending dot of glue, wanting him to make the concession.

She dropped the pump and left it with its mate just where it had fallen. Jeff had done that, too, leaving shoes, clothes, towels, wherever they happened to be when he was finished with them. For the first few months of their married life, she'd lovingly ignored the clutter. But after a while, she'd suspected he did it just to annoy her.

With a sigh, Paige unzipped her dress. She tried not to think about the fact that Jeff had once lived here with her. She'd changed the wallpaper, bought new furniture, replaced the pictures on the bedside table. The whole house was different, but still there were moments when the memories were vivid. Paige supposed she should have known tonight would be one of those times. After seeing him, how could she have expected to come home and forget?

A hot bath helped ease her tension, but still she was restless and Paige knew there was no point in trying to sleep. Instead, she pulled on an old cotton robe and went to sit outside on the deck.

The April night was warm with just a hint of left-over dampness from a morning shower. The air felt good against her skin and it was scented with the fresh, clean fragrance of new grass. Pressing her palms flat against the redwood railing, she closed her eyes and listened to the night song surrounding her—the evening quiet that stirred softly with indistinguishable sounds, the muffled barking of a dog, and the distant hum of traffic.

A car engine vibrated against the hushed, sleepy silence in the neighborhood. It came closer and stopped. Paige listened intently, every nerve pulled taut, but when she heard a car door close, she released her breath in a shaky sigh. It was Jeff. She knew even before his footsteps echoed on the brick path at the side of the house. When he rounded the corner and pushed open the small, redwood gate, she turned.

Jeff caught the movement and froze in place, his heart slamming against his rib cage. Silhouetted by the kitchen light behind her, Paige was a cameo of dusk and ivory. His throat ached with her loveliness. Even though it was difficult to see distinctly in the darkness, he remembered how she looked in various degrees of light and he knew how her dark hair picked up the gleam of sunshine and softened with the sheen of moonlight. Slowly, he settled the gate latch into place, never taking his eyes from her. What in the hell was he doing? He had no right to be here.

"I didn't mean to frighten you," he offered in lieu of explanation.

"I wasn't frightened."

"You weren't?"

She shook her head. "I recognized the slam of the car door."

"It's a different car."

"But the same impatient driver."

Jeff pushed a hand into his pocket. "Not quite the same."

She shrugged a reluctance to argue. "Would you like to join me on the deck? Or are you planning to keep your distance?"

"That sounds like a loaded question."

"It isn't." She turned, casting her face in shadow, and he took a forward step. "I'm saving those until you get within shooting range."

That gave him momentary pause, she noticed, but still he took the stairs like a pro wrestler who knew his business. He surprised her a little by coming to the middle of the deck instead of choosing a corner, but she resolutely stood her ground. Or at least she stood as resolutely as her quivering knees would allow. Her breathing was shallow and her pulse erratic, but aside from that, she felt oddly confident. She didn't know why he had come, but it didn't seem to make any difference.

"This is nice." He indicated the deck with a gesture before crossing his arms at his chest. "When did you have it built?"

"Last summer. I thought it made a nice addition to the house."

His lips tightened. "I thought you'd have sold this house by now."

"I have to live somewhere."

"That attitude's a bit jaded for you, isn't it, Paige?"

With a subtle arch of her brow, she met his skeptical look. "Would you rather hear me say that I couldn't bear to sell it? That I wanted to mourn our marriage in familiar surroundings?"

It was on the tip of his tongue to ask if she had mourned, but pride pressed his mouth into a frown. "I didn't intend to upset you."

"You didn't?"

"Of course not," he snapped, irritated by her composure as much as by her question. "I don't want to get into an argument with you."

"Oh." The truth was he *did* want to argue. Paige knew that even if Jeff didn't. There were too many unresolved emotions between them and a quarrel would ease the tension, pave the way for discussion. But not tonight. Maybe never. She brushed at the wispy bangs on her forehead. "Why did you come, Jeff?"

His pause was experimental. "I just wanted to make sure you arrived safely."

"After two years of not caring? I'm not gullible enough to swallow that one, Jeff. Not from you."

"I didn't really think you would, but that is part of the reason."

"And the other part?"

"Curiosity, I suppose." He looked across the lawn, trying to be honest with himself and a little less than truthful with her. "When I left the hotel, I intended to go straight to the apartment—which, by the way, is very comfortable. Thanks for making the arrangements for me."

"Don't thank me. Cathy Samuels takes care of personnel and personnel-related problems now. She handles all the apartment and car rentals, as well as anything else a visiting VIP might need."

"I thought you were in charge of personnel."

"Not anymore. Edward decided I needed a change, which was a polite way of insisting I spend some time learning about other departments. At the moment, I'm vice-president in charge of sales." She smiled wryly and Jeff's heart went to his throat in wistful response. "That's quite an impressive title for someone who acts as a buffer zone between the salesmen and the rest of the world, isn't it?"

Loosening his tie with a tug of his hand, Jeff relaxed against the railing. "The price of experience."

"Yes." Paige slipped her hands into the patch pockets of her robe. "You were right, Jeff. I wish I hadn't dropped out of college."

"Go back."

"For what? A business degree I don't want?"

"For the speech pathology training you do want."

She sighed. "Things are always black and white for you, Jeff. Randall Electronics is my father's legacy to me. It's my responsibility."

"It's your inheritance, Paige, but you're letting it become your handicap."

It was an old argument, one they'd had many times before. Only in the past few months had she been able to admit he had had some valid points. It was becoming harder to justify the sacrifices she'd made to loyalty. It was becoming even harder to understand why she'd made them in the first place.

This time, Jeff sighed. "Still as stubborn as ever, aren't you? A little more independent, maybe, but just as—"

"I thought you didn't want to argue." She took a couple of steps away, suddenly uncomfortable with his nearness. "Let's go back to why you came."

His shrug was a master of understatement. "I had an impulse to drive past the house. I saw the kitchen light and stopped to . . ." He had no clear idea of why he'd done anything he had done all evening, from going to the awards presentation to standing on this deck. How could he explain the sudden compulsion to see her, to talk to her? ". . . to check on you," he finished lamely.

"At least be honest, Jeff. You stopped to prove you could. You wanted to establish your indifference to me, this house, and anything else that might tie you to our past. And most of all, you wanted me to understand that your acceptance of the job as consultant with Randall Electronics has nothing to do with me."

"But *most of all*, that would be a lie . . . wouldn't it, Paige?" He thought seriously about taking off his jacket, but it seemed important somehow to keep it on. "Just how many strings did you pull to get this job 'opportunity' for me?"

"Your consulting firm was highly recommended."

"By whom?"

"Does that matter? You're the most qualified man for the position."

"I'm sure not everyone agreed."

Her chin lifted a nonchalant half-inch. "I didn't ask for opinions."

"Ah, a royal edict. Isn't that a bit tough on company management?" The silence lengthened and Jeff exhaled a slow breath. "Do you think it was worth the risk?"

"You accepted the job," she said, turning in profile, innocently alluring in the soft light. Or maybe it wasn't innocent at all. Jeff looked away, but his gaze was drawn again to admire the shadowed silhouette of her body.

"You know it isn't that simple, Paige."

"It is, Jeff. I don't know what happened to the NaeComp specification sheets, but I know you didn't take them and—"

"Such blind faith in my integrity." His voice was suddenly crisp and cynical, his gaze narrow and accusing. "A little late, Paige. Just a damn bit too late."

"If that were true, you wouldn't be here. You believe there's a chance to find out what really happened two years ago. I believe so, too, and together we can—"

"Oh, no." He straightened, preparing for opposition. "There is no 'together we can,' Paige. I needed your help then. I don't need it now."

She swallowed hard. "You wouldn't be project manager for the Tri-Star contract without my help."

He turned abruptly, bracing a fist against the redwood rail. She was right, of course, but he resented the way she pointed it out. Paige always had been able to rattle the windows of his most secret insecurity—even now, when there was no logical reason for him to feel that way. "Did I forget to thank you?" he asked caustically, and was immediately sorry he'd let her see his annoyance.

Paige hesitated and then walked to his side. "Jeff, I'm sorry. I know that doesn't mean a whole lot to you now, but this job, it was the only way I could see to—to set things right."

"Why should that suddenly be important? You weren't overly concerned about it then."

"How would you know? You didn't give me much of an opportunity to tell you how I felt about anything. You just left and told me I could file for divorce. You weren't coming back. Period. End of discussion."

"Paige. . . ." He wanted to explain, wanted to open the discussion. But what would that accomplish? If she had only believed in him then, felt just a measure of the faith she was trying to convince him she felt now. "We never learned the art of discussion, you know that. We talked, but when it came to things that really mattered, we didn't know how to listen. Maybe we just didn't love each other enough."

He couldn't believe that! She reached for his arm. "But, Jeff, you don't—" His eyes came to her in the stillness, as quiet and dark as the evening. The protest died on her lips as she recognized a sweet and once familiar yearning. Oh, God! She wanted to be in his arms again. She needed to feel the warmth and strength and wonder only his touch could bring to her. It had been so long, so achingly long.

Awareness throbbed in the silence. A siren wailed in the distance and, overhead, leaves rustled in the wake of an evanescent breeze. Paige stood, afraid to move, caught in the spell of memory. She was lost in his nearness, in the faint scent of his fragrance. His name was a whisper that parted her lips as she lifted her face to his; her step toward him was unhesitating, eager.

Paige had no idea if he met her halfway, if her arms embraced him first, or if his hands initiated the reunion of past desires and present tensions. There was a moment, a fleeting remembrance of other nights when he had held her, caressed her, loved her. A soft sound murmured low in her throat, but she didn't know if it was born of loneliness or of hope. Jeff remained still, only the restless movement of his fingers against her waist revealing his indecision. His expression gave away nothing of what he was feeling, of the questions running through his mind. But she knew.

Her palm moved to his cheek and trembled as she touched him—a touch so well remembered, so desperately missed. Deep inside her, a melting heat traced the path of her longing. At the back of his head, her fingertips renewed acquaintance with the texture of thick, tawny hair and applied a subtle pressure, urging him to bend to her waiting lips.

Jeff resisted no longer. He brought his mouth to hers quickly, capturing the soft yielding warmth of her with a touch both demanding and tender. He couldn't hold her close enough, couldn't stop his tongue from seeking to rediscover the moist, tempting recesses of her mouth. His reason dissolved into reckless desire. It had always been so with Paige—this flaring of passion that defied logic, mocked his will, and culminated in an oddly gentle surrender.

But not this time.

He wanted nothing more than to lift her in his arms and carry her into the house, to the bedroom where he had lain with her so many times before. His body ached with need and on another night perhaps he wouldn't have denied it. But now. . . .

He drew away slowly, supplementing his resolve with long, steady breaths. Her eyes met his in contented wonder, as if she had discovered a secret. It was dangerous to hold her any longer, he knew that, and yet his arms were reluctant to let her go. After two years, he hadn't thought it would be possible to want her so badly. He hadn't dreamed he could still be drawn by the look in her eyes, by the creamy softness of her skin, by his own helpless longings.

Disgusted by his weakness, he forced his arms to his sides and stepped back from temptation, but when she followed, he put his hands on her shoulders and held her at a distance. For a seemingly endless moment, he looked into the questioning blue of her eyes and knew he couldn't intentionally hurt her, no matter how deeply he'd been hurt by her.

"Paige . . ." It was a hoarse whisper, unworthy and unconvincing. He tried again. "Paige, indifference is beyond my ability. There's always been an attraction between us. I suppose that isn't going to change. But I don't want you to misunderstand. If you invite me to your bed, I'll probably accept. If you expect more than that, you're going to be disappointed."

The breath she took was sharp, the flicker of pain in her eyes was quickly extinguished. He could almost believe it had been a trick of the shadows. At least, he might have believed it if he hadn't known her so well. She would be angry now. She would tell him to leave. And that would be better, make everything easier. For her. For him. He waited, his heart heavy with memories.

She wanted to be angry, but two years had altered her perspective, shown her how little anger accomplished. If she had any chance at all to win Jeff's love again, pride would have to go. Not really such a great sacrifice when she considered the sweetness of the last few minutes. He wasn't indifferent. That was a starting place.

"I'll keep that in mind, Jeff. But I think I'd like for you to leave now. We both have some things to think over."

He looked momentarily surprised and . . . perhaps a bit regretful. Paige couldn't discern a hint of either reaction, though, in his quiet good night. As he left her and made his way to the gate, she watched him, absorbing the sight of him, the compelling sensuality of his movements. He didn't look back, and when she heard the slam of the car door, Paige wondered how many more times she could bear to watch him leave.

CHAPTER THREE

"How the hell does Phillip Marlowe do it?" Jeff muttered as he scored a heavy pencil line across the yellow legal pad. There had to be a standard operating procedure, a rule of thumb to follow in piecing together a two-year-old riddle. He frowned and combed impatient fingers through his hair. He wasn't cut out for detective work.

Tapping the pencil lead against the paper, he read through the list of employees who had worked at Randall Electronics two years before and who were either still in management positions or who had left the company for other employment since the time of the theft. It hadn't taken long to compile the names. Deciding what he should do with the information was taking considerably longer.

A suspicious nature would have been an asset, Jeff supposed. Still, logic told him that one of the people on his list had stolen the NaeComp spec sheets. It didn't matter that he couldn't visualize anyone on the list as a corporate thief. What mattered was that *he* hadn't stolen the papers; therefore someone else had.

Opportunity was one criterion. Access to classified information was another. And motive—there always had to be a motive. He leaned back in the chair, trying to blend his thoughts with a plan of action. The list would have to be narrowed, but he just didn't know where to begin.

The phone rang a sharp intrusion and, glad for the interruption, Jeff answered. "Lawrence."

"Welch here." Toby's voice was crisply amused. "The office isn't the same without you, kid. It's actually pleasant around here. Even the receptionist is smiling these days. How long will you be away?"

"About twenty years at the rate I'm progressing now," Jeff said.

"What? Don't tell me Boy Wonder is having trouble with a simple production schedule."

Jeff grinned at the jab. The difference in their ages was insignificant, but Toby liked to point out his few months edge on maturity every now and again. "The production work is going well. It's the sleuthing that's giving me gray hair."

"Better gray than falling out."

"Well, I suppose that's true, but not much of a consolation."

"So, the mystery is still a mystery, huh?" Toby cleared his throat. "And is the ex-wife giving you trouble too?"

"No," Jeff said quickly. "She stays out of my way for

the most part." But she had given him plenty of sleepless nights, just the same. The memory of the midnight kiss had been the focus of more than one restless dream during the past two weeks. He began to trace the lines on the legal pad with the pencil lead. "Her department doesn't have a lot to do with this project, which is probably best for both of us."

"Oh, absolutely. That eases your worry about getting involved with her again."

"I've never worried about getting involved with her, Toby. You know that."

"Right. You were worried she might *think* you wanted to get involved with her. Which, of course, is ridiculous."

Jeff knew his agreement would lack conviction, but a protest would allow more friendly teasing. And he couldn't handle more. He wasn't sure he'd handled this very well. "Is everything going well at the office?" he asked, changing his tone and the subject. "Are we still solvent?"

"What kind of question is that? Do you think for one minute that I can't balance the checkbook? That's why we hired the bookkeeper, remember? What a dragon! I'll never forgive you for hiring that woman, Jeff. She's—" Toby's voice continued, but Jeff lost track of the words as Paige entered his office.

She smiled, a hesitant, timid sort of greeting, and stood for a moment just inside the doorway. Her hair was different today, he noted, feathered back at the temples and held away from her face by two red

.el combs, one on either side. The vivid color ɞtled against the sable darkness of her shoulder-length hair, creating drama simply by contrast. She wore something red, but he barely glanced at her clothes, acknowledging instead the overall mood she projected: warm, confident femininity. He'd always admired that about her. No matter what she did or what clothes she wore, she managed to look comfortable, classy, and totally a woman.

And once she had been his woman.

"Busy?" She mouthed the question, not wanting to interrupt anything important, but unwilling to drop the folders on his desk and leave. After all, she'd spent the past half hour loitering in the hall, waiting to run—strictly by accident, of course—into the mail clerk. It had been the only legitimate reason she could think of to see Jeff and she needed a reason, legitimate or otherwise.

It was crazy, really, to think that after two years of separation she couldn't control the need to be near him. She was hungry just to look at him. She ached with the longing to hold him in her arms. In the two weeks since he'd come to her house, she had fought the same battle day after day. But today she'd lost.

When he motioned for her to come in, she walked to the side of his desk. Holding his mail close in the crook of her arm, she waited, glad that he was preoccupied with a phone call. It gave her an opportunity to observe him, to renew an intimacy of visual touch that once had been her right. She hadn't forgotten the way he looked, but she hadn't fully remembered the effect he had on her. Now, just standing close, she felt an inner excitement. It was partly nerves, she knew, but there was more—the scintillating awareness of mutual attraction, the anticipation of a touch, a look, a message unspoken but understood. She had been very young the first time she'd felt it. She hadn't appreciated the uniqueness, hadn't known it was a special response to a special person—Jeff.

He moved his arm as he said something into the telephone. His voice rippled pleasurably through her senses, reminding her of the husky caress of his breath against her skin. She had to stop this; had to put the memories in perspective. Shifting her gaze from his hand, she looked at the scribbled notes on the legal pad.

It was difficult to decipher, but slowly she realized what he was doing. A list of Randall employees. That must have taken some time, she thought. And determination. It cheered her to know he was thinking about the theft, but she wanted so badly to help, to at least share her ideas with him. When he leaned forward to replace the receiver, she reached for the pad and lifted it in her hand. In careful distraction, she lowered the mail to a corner of his desk while she read the list of names.

"Paige," Jeff spoke calmly, with a hint of tension in his voice, "you shouldn't be—"

"Why not?" She kept reading. "I have as much interest in this as you do."

"I doubt that. You don't even know what that is. Now, give me the—"

"Don't be patronizing. Of course I know what it is *and* I know what you're doing. I can help, Jeff. Please let me."

He pulled the yellow pad from her grasp and placed it on the desk again. Reaching for the pencil, he avoided meeting her eyes. "It's nothing, Paige. Just idle activity."

He drew a line down the paper, for emphasis, she supposed. She wished he would look at her. If only he'd concede her right to be interested, her need to help. "Hasn't there already been too much pretense, Jeff? The chances of finding out what happened to those spec sheets are slim, but I know you're going to try. All I'm asking is that you allow me to try too."

The pencil rolled beneath his fingers, a subtle give-away of his tension. Her heart filled with tender concern and her throat tightened with a familiar longing to soothe him. She'd always wanted to take care of him. He hadn't had a happy childhood, too many problems, not enough love. During their marriage she had tried to compensate, to give him all that he'd missed. But she had given too much and, in a flare of independence, he had left her. This time, she would be more careful.

More than anything at the moment, Jeff wished he could deny that he needed her help. But in going over the list, in thinking about the same facts again and again, it had become apparent that he did need help, and Paige could provide assistance as well as a different point of view. But he hated to admit it and he hated to allow her even that small part of his thoughts, even though he didn't see any other way to make any progress. He would just have to be careful.

"Paige," he said, his voice low and restrained, "I don't want you to feel obligated to help. What happened—well, it was as much my fault as anyone's. I'm not sure I *should* try to unravel the theft now, after all this time. But I certainly don't think you should get involved."

"I am involved, Jeff." She said it quietly but had never been more vehement. "That isn't going to change."

He met her eyes, seeking a common ground, a hint of understanding. Paige didn't know if he found it, but she returned his look with steady composure. There was too much at stake now to reveal any doubts she harbored. He needed her and God knew how very much she needed him.

"If we—" He paused, choosing his words with obvious care. "If we work together on this, Paige, you could get . . . hurt."

It was a warning and her heart received the message. He offered no hope of a reconciliation. He would be polite, friendly, he would accept whatever she offered. But if she expected love in return . . . A cold knot of regret tightened her stomach. Hurt? Yes, it was more than possible, but that was the risk she would have to run. "I know," she whispered. "What can I do to help?"

The corners of his mouth pulled taut, then relaxed with resignation. His gaze left her and she was lonely. "I hardly think this is an appropriate place for discussion, Paige. Why don't we have dinner together?"

She nodded consent. "My house?"

Brown eyes flashed to blue eyes and awareness singed the air around her. "I think my apartment would be safer."

"Safer?" She'd meant to sound light, as if she didn't understand his meaning. But he stifled her attempt with a look and the certain knowledge that whatever happened between them on the surface, he would not allow her to forget the irreconcilable differences between their hearts.

She swallowed and nodded again, her throat too dry for words.

"All right." His tone was crisp, as was his smile. "Tonight, seven o'clock at my apartment. Shall I pick you up?"

"I can find the way." She turned to leave, hesitated, and turned back. "Jeff, I . . ."

The curve of his lips softened in silent understanding. "I know, Paige. I know."

Music mellowed the drab decor of Jeff's apartment and had much the same effect on her mood. In fact, Paige thought, a glass of wine and another bite of egg roll would just about mellow her past the point of prudence. But Jeff didn't offer wine and Paige stoically refused the egg roll. The music, however, was allowed to do its melancholy best.

Across the table, Jeff occasionally caught her eye, but didn't linger long enough to acknowledge the tension. Paige had been aware of it since her arrival. Like the thickness in the air that heralds a coming storm, it had surrounded her the moment the apartment door closed, shutting her into privacy with Jeff.

There seemed so little to say. She could hardly compliment his taste when he'd had nothing at all to do with choosing either the apartment or the furnishings inside. And she found it difficult to simply blurt her thoughts about the theft into the void of awkward silence. So she'd eaten with as much concentrated effort as a carry-in Chinese dinner would allow. But the music, the old songs to which she and Jeff had listened hour upon hour . . . yes, the music was definitely getting to her.

"More?" he asked, extending the plate of glazed chicken.

She shook her head, ruefully eyeing some rice she'd dropped on the table. "Do you remember the time I cooked—?" Her voice broke, not knowing suddenly whether to laugh or cry. So many times had been shared with Jeff in an apartment much like this one—good times, loving times.

"A whole week of rice," he said, picking up her train of memory as smoothly as the stereo changed from song to song. "My punishment for complaining about your cooking."

"Justly deserved too. You really hurt my feelings."

"But you got to me where it counts, Paige. My stomach."

She laughed softly. "Seven ways to prepare instant rice. I could have written a book."

"I should have—" Jeff cut the comment short and rose. "Let's clean up." He began stacking the plates and silverware, and with a carefully concealed sigh, Paige rose to help him. He obviously wasn't interested in reminiscing.

"I see you've learned how to clear off the table." A glass in each hand, she followed him to the kitchen sink. "Living alone certainly develops new skills."

"What makes you think I've lived alone all this time?"

She paused, but only for a moment. "You didn't leave me for someone else, Jeff. And, knowing you, I'd say you haven't been in any rush to replace me."

It aggravated him to admit she was right; it annoyed him even more that she didn't seem particularly worried about being replaced. "Well, you know what they say: 'Once burned, twice shy.' "

Silence greeted his callous quip and he wished he hadn't said it. More than that, he wished it no longer mattered what he said. But he knew, without so much as a glance, that he'd hurt her . . . and it mattered. "I'm sorry, Paige. That was a thoughtless thing to say."

"I wasn't being very thoughtful myself. This is kind of—awkward. Maybe we should forget we used to be married."

She reached past him for a dish towel and he forced his hand not to touch hers. *Forget we used to be married.* God, if he only knew how. "Let's just settle for avoiding personal topics of conversation, all right?"

"Sure." With a shrug, she leaned against the countertop and casually wiped her hands. "Is it okay if I thank you for dinner?"

"It wasn't any trouble." He smiled—just a little. "You're not hard to please, Paige."

She looked at the towel in her hands. "It's nice to know you remember my favorite . . ." Oops, she thought, too personal. Try again. "I'm glad you invited me. I've wanted to see inside this apartment—this apartment *building,* I mean. It's nice. But it isn't that much better than—"

The apartment they'd shared as newlyweds—Jeff knew the comparison she'd stopped herself from making. He'd thought the same thing himself. Their apartment had been smaller, more cramped, but somehow their whole world had fitted nicely inside. With an unnecessarily rough push, he closed the dishwasher. "Do you want some coffee?"

She dropped the towel, then looked surprised to see it on the floor. "No," she said, stooping to pick it up and place it back on the counter. "Why don't we take a look at that list now?"

He accepted her crisp, businesslike tone with a measure of regret. "Let's go into the front room. We'll be more comfortable there." It sounded so cozy, and he couldn't help remembering the times they had made love in that other apartment, in that other lifetime. Abruptly, he moved away from her and from the memories.

He intended to turn off the music, but once in the living room, he couldn't bring himself to eliminate that one remaining link, the one common interest he knew they still shared. Instead he sat on the sofa and leaned forward to open the briefcase which lay on the coffee table. Paige hesitated at one end of the sofa before walking to the other side of the table and sinking, cross-legged, to the floor. As he lifted the legal pad and pushed aside the briefcase, she chuckled softly to herself. The sound was melodic and reminiscently disarming and it touched his heart with helpless longing. "Something funny, Paige?" he asked in quick self-denial.

"Just thinking about . . . oh, nothing. Just thinking."

At that moment he would have given anything to know what she was thinking. He wanted to hear her laugh again, to laugh with her. But that time was past. "I'd prefer to discuss this seriously, if you don't mind."

"Whatever you say, Charlie Chan." Her eyes widened innocently as they met his, then she sobered and dropped her gaze to the tablet in his hand. "So where do we start?"

Jeff sighed a general frustration. "I hoped you could tell me. Frankly, I'm better with computer malfunctions than I am with people's motives."

"What motive could there be except money?" Paige took the list from him and regarded it pensively. "Everyone thought that was *your* motive. The most popular rumor after you left was that I wouldn't finance your business venture, so you got back at me by stealing from my company. Of course, no one ever said that directly to me, but I heard it just the same."

"And did you defend me just the same?"

His voice was raspy, and Paige slowly lifted her eyes to meet the cool brown of his. "You made it pretty difficult to do that, Jeff. There were days when I hated you for leaving me alone to face all the whispers and stares."

"And was it one of those days when you filed for divorce?"

She tried to swallow the bitter taste in her mouth. How could he? How could he dare? "I did only what you wanted me to do, Jeff. And don't bother to—" With closed eyes, she drew a long breath. "I thought you wanted to keep this impersonal."

His stillness indicated a trace of indecision, but when he spoke, he sounded definite. "I do. Let's discuss the people on that list, shall we?"

For a fraction of a second, she wanted to yell at him, tell him she was leaving his dreary apartment, that she didn't care what he did. But she did care. And she couldn't leave. Sighing, she settled more comfortably on the floor and read aloud the first three names. The stereo clicked another record into place and an old love song filtered softly through her tension. She paused, wanting to listen to the lyrics, knowing what a mistake that would be.

"Well?" Jeff asked impatiently. "What do you think?"

Her attention shifted to the list once again. "You could have alphabetized these." At his frown, she tried to concentrate. "It doesn't really matter. First, I suppose, we should try to establish *how* the papers were stolen and then we can figure out who on this list needed quick, tax-free cash badly enough to steal them."

"All of these people had security clearance. Any one of them could have walked out of the vault with the NaeComp file."

"But did they all have the time and opportunity? Edward had the spec sheets in that afternoon meeting, remember?"

"Of course I remember. After the meeting, I was responsible for returning the file to security." The pause was brief, but meaningful. "I did return it, Paige, intact."

The unfairness of that clarification wandered through her like the haunting notes of an oboe singing from the stereo. "I never doubted that you did, Jeff."

She sensed his need to argue, to test her sincerity further, but he didn't. Instead, he clasped his hands and rose to pace the room. "There were approximately three hours in which the papers could have been taken, three hours between the time I checked them into security and the time the vault was closed for the weekend. But you know what it's like on Friday afternoons—everyone clearing off their desks, milling around, talking about plans for the weekend. If ever there's a time when someone could slip into the vault, Friday's the day."

"I suppose it's possible, but I just can't believe—" She tapped the paper with a fingernail. "No, Jeff, it has to be someone on this list. Who else would realize the value of those sheets? No one outside of management would have known the overall potential for that microchip, or what company might be in the market for such specific information."

He stopped pacing to look down at her. "All right, then see if you can narrow the list to a manageable size."

She did in less than fifteen minutes. Jeff was surprised at the results, but not by her method. Paige relied on intuition and she crossed out names with little more than a sentence explanation. "Too conservative," she said about one. "Family man," she said of another. "Religious scruples," "unimaginative," and "ridiculous" were her comments as the pencil lead snaked through the possibilities.

Jeff didn't know whether to sigh or smile as he

watched her. It was a familiar ambiguity, closely associated with all his feelings toward Paige. The last thing he should have done was to have invited her to his apartment, but the last thing he wanted now was for her to leave. His fingers ached with the longing to tangle her dark hair, but he kept them safely at his sides. He would have liked to tell her how beautiful she was, but that might . . . No, he didn't want to think where that might lead. In the end, it could only lead him in a circle . . . a pointless, bittersweet circle. He sighed.

Glancing up, Paige smiled but won no response. "There," she said as she handed the tablet to him. "This ought to give us something to work with. See what you think."

Jeff took the list, but his mind wasn't on stolen papers and hidden motives. There were six names left on the list, four men and two women, six people who might be responsible for the theft that shadowed his reputation. He knew he should make some comment, some indication that he agreed or disagreed with her choices. But he just nodded and tossed the pad back onto the coffee table. "I'll do some investigating and let you know what I find out."

Paige considered the nonchalant tone of his voice before raising her eyes to his. "You think I'm wrong, don't you, Jeff? You don't believe we're going to get to the bottom of this. I'm beginning to wonder if you even want to."

He was beginning to wonder the same thing. The

longer she stayed in his apartment, the less he cared who had stolen the spec sheets. "Damn it, Paige, I don't know what to believe. It's been two years. Maybe that's just too long."

Too long. Too long. Her mind superimposed the phrase over the melody playing softly in the background. There was an element of timing in all of life, that one moment when everything could go right or wrong, when hope flowered or died. And she had to follow her instincts, her gut feeling that this was the right time, that it hadn't been too long. She wouldn't let it be. "It will work out, Jeff. You'll see."

He didn't think so. She could tell by the tension at the corners of his mouth and the rigid set of his shoulders. "I'd ask you to dance, but my foot's asleep," she said to lighten the heaviness of her spirit, but the tingling pinpricks along her ankle were painfully truthful. One careful movement at a time, she shifted her weight and flexed her foot.

Unexpectedly, Jeff smiled and offered his help via an outstretched hand. "You should know better than to sit like that. Here, be careful. You can turn your ankle—"

"Stop fussing." She stood, balancing between her good foot and Jeff's supporting hand. "If you don't want to dance, just say so."

He answered by pulling her into his arms and beginning to sway in time with the music. The tingling sensation in her foot was instantly secondary to the awareness cascading through her. He held her close, providing a gentle strength for her momentary weakness. She hoped he didn't realize that his very closeness caused a far more unsettling debility in her knees.

"Better?" The movement of his lips against her hair caressed her with a relaxing familiarity. He was asking about her foot, she knew, but at that particular moment Paige hardly remembered she had feet. "Hmmm," she answered vaguely and let her hands slide from his shoulders to encircle his neck. Her body swayed with his, the rhythm becoming a low, steady heartbeat, an old sweet song that she knew so very well.

When had she first danced with him? Oddly, she couldn't recall the time or the place. Only that he had held her before as he was holding her now. It had been wonderful then. It was better now. Perhaps because she had missed him. Perhaps because their closeness was a transient feeling, destined to fade when the music stopped.

She wanted the song to go on and on, never ending, yet a restlessness spun in widening spirals inside her. Her body craved the release to be found in his; her heart longed to express emotion in a thousand loving touches. But how could she bear to love him, knowing he was no longer hers, realizing how truly she had lost him?

The music ebbed into silence, but Jeff kept dancing. He held her close and wanted to pull her even deeper into his embrace. She fitted so perfectly against him. It was madness to want her, sheer insanity to believe anything but heartache could come of it. Yet for those few moments he wished that time might melt into memories and again become the early, happy days of their marriage. He hadn't expected more than her love then. He hadn't needed more than the soft sweetness of her smile.

But Paige had wanted more. Her expectations always had eluded his understanding, and even now he could only guess at her motives and at what she wanted from him. And what did he want from her? Physical satisfaction? Yes, it was as simple as that. He wasn't about to let emotion cloud the issue. Realizing that she was smiling up at him, Jeff paused and braced his resolve against the enchanting loveliness in his arms.

"Aren't you going to put on another record?" she asked.

"That's up to you, Paige."

The choice was hers, she thought, as she drowned slowly in the whirlpool between recklessness and reason. Jeff offered neither encouragement nor discouragement, and she knew he would accept her decision without comment. And, in the end, it was that very distance that helped her move away from the warm circle of his arms.

"Maybe some other time, Jeff." It was a lackluster response to an impossible situation. She wanted him. He wanted her. The attraction was as strong as ever, but pride stood guard and cast a larger-than-life shadow between their hearts. With a sigh, Paige gathered her belongings and walked to the door. "Thanks for dinner. It was . . ."

A wistful longing clustered in her throat and she finished the thought with a semblance of a smile. Her hand reached for the doorknob and fanned empty air. Jeff stepped to her assistance and opened the door, the hairs on his arm brushing her skin with heightened awareness.

"Thank you for wanting to help, Paige," he said politely, hoping against hope she would have no idea of the effort that politeness required. He didn't want her to leave, but the words asking her to stay would not come. An eternity passed as they stood in cautious silence, but then abruptly it ended. Paige turned. "Good night, Jeff."

He watched her walk away and did not close the door until her footsteps had faded into the night. Then he restacked the records on the stereo and stared out the small, apartment-sized window as the music played on and on and on.

CHAPTER FOUR

Sandi Winners . . . wasn't.

Jeff had always thought her name was deceptively inappropriate and after two years his opinion remained unchanged. Oh, he'd admit that she was attractive and she was one hell of a good engineer, but her name did not suit her image. Her coloring was a far cry from sandy and her personality was an equal distance from winning.

Jeff had never been able to pinpoint exactly what it was about her that bothered him, but Sandi—spelled carefully and consistently with an *i* by anyone who had ever made the mistake of misspelling it—made him uncomfortable.

Even now, although she was standing safely a desk width away from him, Jeff sensed that she was plotting to move closer. Maybe it was the strategic location of the unbuttoned buttons on her blouse. Or maybe it was the way she kept licking her lips and smiling. Or maybe it was simply because he was about to ask her out to dinner.

No doubt that was the real source of his discomfort,

he thought, as he waited for a break in the one-sided conversation. She had come into his office to "consult" with him about a project on which she was working, but in slightly less than a half hour, she hadn't once asked his opinion. He was going to hate spending an evening with her, but her name was on Paige's reduced list of possible suspects and he didn't know a better way to get information from Sandi than by asking her out.

"Are you busy tomorrow night?" Jeff realized it was not an enthusiastic invitation, but he tried to cover up with a hopeful smile. She'd never know he was hoping her social calendar was solidly booked. "I thought we might go out for dinner."

Sandi looked as if she'd been caught totally off-guard. If it hadn't been for that neckline, Jeff might have believed it too. "You're kidding," she said. "You're asking me—?"

Her laughter was softly feminine and sounded genuine. Jeff began to wonder if she could possibly have unfastened those buttons by accident. *Stupid thought, Lawrence,* he told himself as he kept a rueful frown from settling on his lips. He definitely was out of practice with this sort of thing. "Would you like to go?"

"I'd love to." She straightened in slow motion as if she were afraid a quick movement might startle him. "But I can't."

Jeff's emotions swung from regret to relief, then

evened out somewhere in between. "Oh, that's too bad. Maybe another—"

"Unless. . . ."

God, he hated to ask. "Unless?"

"Unless you'd want to take me to the party." Her smile grew eager. "You see, I've been invited to a small get-together and if you'd care to—"

"I wouldn't feel right about crashing a party." He would get out of this somehow, he vowed. Sandi Winners couldn't possibly give him that much valuable information. "We'll just make it some other—"

"No, really, Jeff. It would be fine. Paige said it would be all right if I brought a date."

All sense of humor took wing and left him ill-tempered. *"Paige?* This small get-together is at my—at Paige's house?"

To her credit, Sandi did look a trifle embarrassed. "Oh, I guess that would be awkward for you, wouldn't it? I'm sorry, I didn't think . . . well, you know, you and Paige act so friendly, it seemed like a good idea." Sandi reached across the desk to pat his hand. "But I understand perfectly why you wouldn't want to go—" The embarrassment lost itself in a self-conscious smile.

Try as he might, Jeff couldn't see any reason for smiling. "I didn't say I wouldn't go. In fact, it's the best 'invitation' I've had all day."

Sandi pressed her lips into a tight line and, inexplicably, Jeff felt guilty at taking advantage. *Taking advantage?* What was he thinking? He'd just been maneuvered into taking a "date" to a party at his ex-wife's house. A disconcerting idea occurred to him. "Is this a couples type of—" He swallowed an ounce of pride. "Will Paige have a date?"

Jeff was unprepared for the guilty expression that rounded Sandi's dark eyes. "Oh, Jeff, I'm sorry. Ordinarily, I just wouldn't go, but when you asked me out to dinner, I saw the opportunity and I . . ." She stumbled into silence and he tried to appear less confused than he actually was. "Gary will be there," she said, as if that explained everything.

"Gary." Jeff repeated the name with an inane nod and tried to control the anger rising like a hot air balloon inside him. Gary Glendenning. Edward's son and Jeff's onetime rival for Paige's affections. Apparently, Gary hadn't given up hope. Apparently, he had good reason not to. Jeff frowned. "What time shall I pick you up?"

"You mean you still want to take me to the party?" Sandi's tone took on a wistful warmth. "Even though I'd rather be—even though it wouldn't be fair to you?"

Jeff didn't know or care what she was talking about, but he promised himself he'd spend some time figuring it out just as soon as he could think calmly again. At the moment, he couldn't consider anyone except Paige . . . and he was not in the mood to consider *her* calmly. "What time?" he repeated, impatient to give rein to his anger.

Sandi suggested seven-thirty and Jeff made a note

of her address. When she started to tell him where Paige lived, he quelled her confiding voice with a weary glance. Once Sandi turned to leave, he was attacked by another, stronger sense of guilt. A little gallantry was definitely in order. Not to mention plain good manners. "Sandi, thank you. I'll look forward to tomorrow."

She smiled—a shy, pleasant sort of smile—and Jeff thought perhaps he'd misjudged her before. Maybe there was more to Sandi Winners than bleached out hair and a few unbuttoned buttons. Not that he particularly wanted to find out. He'd much prefer to find out what relationship Paige enjoyed with Gary Glendenning.

Jeff paced to the file cabinet and pulled open a drawer, thinking that he just might be tempted to strangle Paige if she "enjoyed" it. Jerking out a manila folder, he placed his palm against the drawer. But before temper could send it slamming into the file, he drew a deep breath and won control. The drawer slid quietly into place and Jeff regarded it in somber contemplation. It would have felt good to vent his frustration, but it was pointless to go around slamming doors and file-cabinet drawers.

Two years and look at you, he told himself. The divorce, the disillusionment, the time away from her—none of it had made any difference. Paige sashayed back into his life and the first thing he knew, he was angry. My God, he had no right to be angry. She wasn't married to him anymore. What she did was none of his business. And if she wanted to date a loser like Gary Glendenning, well . . . who was Jefferson Lawrence to tell her she couldn't?

But when had that ever stopped him? That was the thing about Paige. He was never on an even keel with her. Emotions he hadn't known existed commanded his reactions whenever she was anywhere around—anger, passion, frustration, longing. No one else could make him feel so helplessly intense.

Sitting in the chair, Jeff laid the file on the desk blotter before him. He drummed his fingers against the manila folder and thought back over the evening in his apartment. Everything Paige had said as well as the quickly disguised yearning in her expression had led him to believe she wanted him. And God knew how badly he wanted her. So where did Gary Glendenning fit in?

Jeff opened the file, but stared sightlessly past it. On the other hand, maybe he was being unfair to her. He'd discouraged her as often as the opportunity presented itself. He'd tried to make it clear that he had no interest in reconciliation, no intention of letting her get close to his heart again.

And yet, here he sat, unable to concentrate on his work, a hollow feeling grinding away in his stomach at the mere *thought* of Paige with Gary Glendenning. Jeff had warned her that if she expected too much, she would be disappointed, that if she wanted more than he was willing to offer, she could get hurt.

He would do well to heed that warning himself.

Even the embers of a dying flame held enough fire to burn. And he had enough scars to last a lifetime. But as he turned his attention to the information in the file, he admitted that nothing short of a national disaster would keep him away from that party.

The idea struck him, halfway between Sandi's apartment and Paige's house, that the evening promised to be a bit more awkward than he'd imagined. Out of the blue, Jeff remembered some gossip from several years before. According to the office grapevine, Sandi had, at one time, had an affair with Gary Glendenning, a rather torrid affair, too, if Jeff recalled the rumor correctly.

He glanced at Sandi from the corner of his eye and mentally shook his head. She was certainly attractive, in an inexpensive sort of way. Not that she looked cheap, Jeff decided. Her clothes were silky, slinky, and stylish, but she had a little too much shape and not enough charisma to wear them well. And she didn't seem to recognize the difference between an overreaction and an appropriate response.

Sandi and Gary. It seemed a curious match to Jeff. And if she still harbored some tender feelings for Gary, that would explain her eagerness to attend the party with an escort.

Tightening his grip on the wheel, Jeff ignored the scratchy feel of her fingernails against his neck. He shifted uncomfortably and Sandi moved her hand to rest along the top of the car seat. "You're not nervous, are you?" she asked.

"No." Jeff didn't think *nervous* quite summed up his feelings at the moment. *Half-witted* came to mind, along with several other pithy phrases. But he hesitated to say anything about his reservations in front of Sandi. "Just looking for a place to park," he said instead.

Considering the way she kept touching him, he ought to find one fast, he thought, even though they were at least a block and a half from Paige's southside home. It was foolish to allow Sandi's comment to rattle his composure. After all, he wasn't actually nervous, just a little apprehensive about the evening ahead. Only an idiot would let himself get caught in such an awkward, impossible situation.

There were cars parked in the driveway of Paige's home, and that annoyed him. Once it had been his privilege to park there; it would never have occurred to him to park anywhere else. But tonight his only option was to wedge his car between a Cadillac and a Volkswagen on the opposite side of the street. Sandi's car door scraped the curb when opened and Jeff winced in irritation.

"Well, we're here," Sandi announced in a bubbly voice, as if she thought the next couple of hours promised to be the most exciting moments of her life.

"Yes." Jeff agreed as he carefully closed the door.

"I didn't tell Paige you were coming. Won't she be surprised?"

"Oh, I doubt it," he answered evenly. "I'm sure that by now Paige is accustomed to expecting the unexpected from you."

Sandi dimpled in pleased acceptance of what she obviously considered a compliment. Jeff had been thinking about Paige's reaction for the past twenty-four hours himself, and he'd concluded that surprise would probably rank at least third on her list of immediate emotions, right behind anger and panic. Oh, he knew she'd be gracious and outwardly polite, but inside . . .

Jeff smiled, anticipating and intending to savor every flash of irritation in her eyes, every nuance of panic in her voice.

But it was Gary Glendenning, with his big-as-Dallas grin, who opened the front door. And it was Sandi whose jaws snapped shut with irritation. The rising panic was left for Jeff and he felt it hit him like a solid fist to the stomach. Where was Paige? And what in hell was she doing letting this cowboy act as if he had every right to welcome *her* guests? His first impulse was to rearrange Gary's face, but his second was much more civilized. "Hello, Gary," he said. "Are you the doorman for this evening?"

"No, he's the door*mat,*" Sandi whispered audibly, tilting a coy and provocative smile to Gary even as she giggled into Jeff's ear and slipped her hand around his arm. "Good evening, Mr. Glendenning. How have you been?"

"Just wonderful, darlin'. How about you?"

Caught between the cowboy drawl and the simpering giggle, Jeff wanted to order them both out of his house and off of his property. But, of course, it wasn't his anymore.

"May we come in?" he asked pointedly, and urged Sandi forward with a gentle tug. Her fingernails were scarring his arm right through his jacket, but he accepted the pressure with good grace and managed to escort her past Gary and into the entryway.

Laughter and music drifted from the back of the house and Jeff looked toward the sound, feeling more displaced than he ever remembered feeling before. This was wrong, all wrong. He knew it even before he saw her, even before the wistful regret in her eyes tucked itself into his heart. There was not an excuse he could offer, no apology that would suffice. And there wasn't any way he could walk away from her now.

"Hello, Paige," he said, but the mending tone was lost to Sandi's sharper vibrato.

"I hope you don't mind, Paige. You did say I could bring a date." The grip on Jeff's arm tightened—or it might have been his own tension that created the stress. "So when Jeff suggested dinner, I invited him to come to the party with me." Sandi cast her look of appeal toward Paige and then let it slide slowly, meaningfully, to Gary.

For his part, Jeff couldn't see anyone but Paige. She appeared quite calm. If he hadn't known her so well, he might not have noticed the whiteness around her lips or the soft creases at her eyes. She was wearing a skirt and blouse, violet and black in color, gypsy casual in style. Jeff swallowed hard at the sight of the low, rounded neckline and the bare satin skin above it. Shiny wings of raven hair curved against her shoulders and he ached to brush it aside and kiss the hollows hidden beneath. How had he survived so long without her?

There hadn't been any other choice.

There still wasn't.

He turned purposefully to give his attention to Sandi, and Paige felt her heart sink to the floor. For a moment, a split second of eternity, she had thought . . .

With a sheltered sigh and a great deal of effort, she invited the newly arrived guests to join the party. As she watched Jeff move into the room, easily making himself at home, her heart settled back into place with a nagging displeasure that escalated with inexplicable and alarming speed. What did he think he was doing? He'd just walked, uninvited, into her home with Sandi Winners—of all people—on his arm.

Paige was angry and that annoyed her. She wanted to tell everyone to go home, to leave her alone with this man who'd once been her husband so that she could *order* him to— It was stupid to even think of venting her frustration on Jeff. She didn't want to argue with him. She didn't even want to be angry with him. Not now, when all she really wanted was to love him.

Paige made her way to the buffet table and checked the trays of hors d'oeuvres. How could she feel so much as a fragment of tenderness for him when he'd put her in this awkward and awful situation? He ought to be hung by his ears for crashing her party. Not that she'd had much enthusiasm for the evening anyway, but now—well, Jeff had made sure the night would be a disaster.

She hadn't wanted to have the get-together in the first place, but the party had been Gary's suggestion, his idea of a way to cheer the leftover moodiness of a long, cold winter. With Jeff present, though, Paige knew her moodiness had only just begun. And if Sandi didn't take her hand off of his sleeve—

Turning her steps to the kitchen, Paige managed to control an urge to slam a cabinet door or two. Jeff was to blame. Didn't he realize how she would feel if he brought another woman to her house, the home he'd once shared? Didn't he understand yet how very much she still cared for him?

"Need some assistance, sweet thing?" Gary followed his offer into the room and Paige tried not to grimace at his term of affection. She'd known him for years, ever since her mother had married Edward, but she'd never gotten used to Gary's endearments. They were trite and unimaginative, not unlike Gary himself. Paige smiled at him in fond acceptance. She'd never understood how Edward could have fathered such a son, and yet there was something about Gary—something deeper than his blustery manner and ever-present grin. He was obnoxiously independent, but she'd never known anyone who she thought needed other people more than he. At one time, she'd dated him almost exclusively because she'd known how much Edward had hoped she and Gary would marry. But of course that was before Jeff. . . .

"I just came in here to—" She had come into the kitchen for perspective, but she wasn't going to explain that to Gary. She shrugged. "I've forgotten, so it must not have been important. We probably should join the party, don't you think?"

He placed a large hand against the doorframe to block her exit. "They're doing fine without us. Let's slip out the back door and have our own little party."

Why were men always suggesting "slipping out the back door"? Paige wondered. Did they think there was something inherently clandestine about the idea? "Thanks, Gary, but I've worked all day getting this party together and I, for one, plan to enjoy it."

"I could plan something you'd enjoy."

Her brows arched doubtfully. "Is that why you invited Sandi and her *date?*"

Gary laughed. "You don't think I'd have breathed a word to Sandi about this party if I'd known she'd bring your ex, do you? She's just trying to make me jealous."

Unfortunately, Paige thought, it wasn't Gary who was affected in that way. "And is she succeeding?"

"Would it bother you if I said yes?"

With a slow shake of her head, Paige lifted his hand away from the doorway and let it drop to his side. "You know the answer to that, Gary. You're a great stepbrother, but—"

"But that's as far as your feelings for me go. I know, Paige. You don't have to keep reminding me."

Oh, yes, she did. At every turn. He was almost as stubborn as Jeff. Without comment, she stepped past Gary and walked across the hallway, pausing at the living room entrance before entering. Gary followed, stopped beside her, and placed his arm around her. If Jeff hadn't chosen that precise moment to glance up and narrow his gaze on the hand at her waist, Paige would simply have ignored the familiarity of the gesture, just as she ignored Gary's corny drawl and his often proprietary manner.

But with that look, a rebellious glimmer of laughter rippled through her. Jeff could think what he liked. And if he chose to spend the evening with a professional blonde wrapped around his arm . . . well, it was no more than he deserved.

"Hello, sugar!" Gary waved to someone across the room. He leaned down and his whisper slid moistly across Paige's ear. "Don't you think we ought to dance, hon? If you don't ask me, someone else will."

Paige clicked her tongue in rueful sympathy. "Life is really rough for you, isn't it, Gary? Why don't I put some more records on the stereo? Then 'sugar' will probably beat a two-step to your side."

"I'd rather dance with you."

She patted his cheek. "You're sweet, Gary, but pushy. Very pushy."

"But think how old Lawrence over there will feel when he sees you in my arms." Gary waggled his eyebrows suggestively. "We might get something stirred up tonight."

Glancing from a corner of her eye, Paige felt the sparks of disapproval radiating in her direction. She was afraid something was already stirring. "Let's just try to enjoy this evening."

"If you insist." Gary's hand left her waist as he straightened. "But don't try too hard. I'm going to keep my eyes on you."

Paige sighed her relief when Gary left her to follow the trail of a beckoning smile. The relief, though, was short-lived. She had hardly edged her way into the room before Jeff was beside her. Bracing herself for an argument, she turned.

"Nice party, Paige," he said pleasantly, putting her even more on guard. "Nice of you to invite me."

She wasn't about to touch that line. "Oh, anytime. Feel free to make yourself at home."

He reached past her to take a glass from the table. "I am. In fact, as I was watching Glendenning nuzzle your ear, I was thinking about the time we—"

"He was just saying—whispering, actually—" She

broke off the explanation as Jeff straightened and slowly grinned.

"Right. Well, as I said, it reminded me of the time he tried to—"

"Jefferson Lawrence, if you do anything—if you so much as crack your knuckles at Gary and try to start something!"

Jeff lifted a hand in self-defense. "Hey, all I said was—"

"I know *what* you said and I remember *distinctly* what happened. And if you think for one minute that I'll stand here and—"

"You look very nice tonight, Paige. New outfit?"

She glanced down and firmed her chin as her eyes returned to his. "Don't try to change the subject, Jeff. I know what you're up to."

"You do?" Carefully, casually, he raised the glass to his lips and drank. "Well, if you think I came here to wrestle with your cowboy and pin him under the coffee table, you're mistaken."

Unbidden, she remembered the original incident and the look on Gary's face. Paige couldn't hold back a smile. "He has quite a few pounds on you now, Jeff. You probably couldn't do it again, anyway."

Tawny brows lifted skeptically. "We're not going to find out tonight. I have other"—his gaze went to Sandi—"things on my mind."

Paige absently took a cracker and bit off a corner. It tasted like salted cotton. "Really? I hadn't noticed."

"Well, I haven't been able to get her to nuzzle my ear yet, but—"

"Don't tell me you've lost your touch."

His fingertips brushed hers, accidentally, it seemed; but as his touch feathered higher, Paige realized how very deliberate it was. Time, breathing, heartbeat—all stopped as Jeff stroked her arm in a quiet, mesmerizing caress. She hated the helpless feeling drifting through her and she wished she had some control over the pulsing need centered low in her stomach. But now, as always, Jeff could melt her logic, her careful reasons, with a mere touch.

"Have I lost it, Paige?" he asked softly.

She knew he didn't need an answer. He knew she wouldn't give one. In mute agreement, they stepped apart, both unsure if the question, and the inevitable answer, should be acknowledged. "Paige, I—" Jeff wanted so badly to explain, to reach out for the common denominator that kept him tied to the past, to her. But his voice faltered, and in the moment of hesitation a guest approached the buffet table and the opportunity was gone.

After a polite introduction and brief exchange of small talk, Jeff returned to Sandi. He didn't leave her company for the rest of the evening, but his thoughts never came close to her. An hour dawdled past and then another. Sandi talked. So did he, but he had no idea what was said by either one of them. He knew every time Paige laughed, though, and he was constantly alert and aware of where she was at any given moment. He was watching when she intercepted Gary on his way toward the coffee table and coaxed him into dancing with her. Jeff didn't like that, but then Paige didn't seem overly thrilled either. Jeff knew she had envisioned a repeat of that long-ago and extremely juvenile wrestling match, but she surely didn't think *he* would behave that way now, did she?

She might, he admitted, but he hoped she was more concerned by what Gary might decide to do. Jeff wondered why he'd ever imagined that Paige could have been unfaithful during their marriage, especially with someone like Gary Glendenning.

And yet, jealousy—that irrational, unquenchable doubt—had caused more arguments, more friction, in their relationship than any other single factor. He had loved Paige deeply, intensely, and yet he'd never trusted her with his most secret feelings. He'd never allowed her to know all of him. And, as it had turned out, it was a good thing. But dissatisfying. Very dissatisfying. Especially when she was dancing with someone else.

It was a relief when the party began to break up, an even greater relief when Sandi told him on the drive to her apartment that she had a splitting headache and couldn't invite him inside for an after-party drink. Jeff hoped he expressed a reasonably flattering disappointment before beating a hasty retreat from her doorway.

The car, with only minimal assistance from him,

found the way back to Paige's house, and he parked in the same spot across the street. Jeff didn't bother with excuses for his conscience. The as-yet-undefined reason he'd returned seemed unimportant when he recognized Gary's low-slung Ferrari still in the driveway. If that cowboy had any thought of staying past his welcome . . .

Jeff's hand went to open the car door and froze as the front door of the house opened. The light from inside pooled through the open doorway and silhouetted Gary's broad shoulders and tall stetson. Jeff strained to see Paige and was rewarded with a glimpse of her as she stood just inside the doorway. His throat ached with the smile that graced her lips, a smile he could only imagine . . . and remember. She had barely said good night earlier when he'd left with Sandi on his arm. There had been no smile then.

Was she smiling now? For Gary? Jeff glanced away from the scene, but just as quickly looked back. He didn't want to, but he had to know what kind of good night Gary received. If Paige kissed him. . . .

She didn't, and Jeff slowly loosened his death grip on the steering wheel as Gary turned and strolled toward the sports car. Even though Paige was already back inside the house, Gary seemed in no hurry to leave and Jeff gritted his teeth as he waited. No clear idea of his own intentions or even of what he was waiting for occurred to him, but Jeff sighed a heartfelt relief when the Ferrari purred loudly and streaked off into the night.

It was not a lack of courage that kept him motionless inside the car. It was not even the fear that she might close the door on him. He supposed he'd known the moment he read the letter offering him this job that temptation would lure him back to her arms. She must have known it too. But after tonight, what would happen? Where would it end?

The questions echoed dully through his thoughts, but weren't strong enough to change his mind. He'd come back to love her, if only for tonight. And love her he would. It was, he realized, the only way to unravel the past. Stolen papers and circumstantial evidence had been just an excuse. The real reason he had left two years before was Paige. And ultimately, the answer for which he now searched would have to come from her.

In the midnight silence, Jeff got out of the car and walked to her door.

CHAPTER FIVE

Paige thought the party would never end, and then she thought Gary would never stop talking about it.

It had been a disaster. There was no other way to describe the evening, no matter what Gary said. Even when she finally closed the door behind him, Paige wondered if the tension in her body would ever ease.

With a long-drawn-out sigh, she slipped off her sandals, lifted her arms, and stretched, bending from side to side. The stereo provided a quiet accompaniment and Paige tried to relax into the music. But the thought of Jeff, the lingering *feel* of his presence in the room, wouldn't release its hold on her.

She had gone through a wide range of emotions in a few short hours. Now all that was left was the restlessness, and the empty confusion of knowing what she wanted, but of not knowing how to get it.

The sound of the Ferrari's powerful engine barely registered in her mind, but the muffled sound of a car door on the street brought her straightening in alert. Her hand sought the support of the wall as her whole body tightened with the effort of listening. There was only silence, or did she hear something? A footstep, perhaps?

Nothing definite . . . and yet she knew, somehow, that Jeff was back. When the knock came, quietly demanding entrance, she wasn't alarmed. Her eyes simply closed in a moment of sweet relief. She shouldn't acknowledge it. She knew she shouldn't even open the door, but how could she not? Her heart refused to recognize the existence of any barrier between her and Jeff . . . not distance or divorce or doors of any kind. Her fingers trembled, her pulse drummed an uneven rhythm of anticipation as she reached for the doorknob.

Jeff raised his hand to knock again, but lowered it slowly as the door opened. His eyes met hers, his breath caught with reckless desire. He was ten times a fool for coming back, and yet at that moment he would gladly have surrendered all the wisdom he possessed or ever hoped to gain just to hold her in his arms, just to love her with the innocence he had lost.

"Hello," he said, because he had to say something.

"Did you forget something?" She lifted her brows with the suggestion.

"No."

"Did Sandi forget something?"

"I wouldn't know."

Paige glanced down at her bare feet, thinking how odd it was that she felt no awkwardness now. By rights, she ought to feel uncomfortable, perhaps even annoyed, by Jeff's return. She felt only a shaky excitement, the unfolding of a fragile hope that had nothing to do with the questions she made herself ask. "Did you find out anything about the spec sheets?"

Jeff grimaced. "I never even thought about it."

He took a step forward and placed a hand on the door. "Invite me in, Paige," he said softly.

The pulsebeat in her throat quickened. "And if I do?"

His eyes held her as his fingers touched her hair and then her cheek. Like a puppet in the hand of the master, she responded to the tug on her heart. She had no power to resist and no reason to try. As if he pulled the strings, her palm lifted to cup his face, to know again the texture of his skin. With the contact came memories and pleasures she hadn't known for far too long. Nights without him had been endless. Now she wished morning would never come.

He kissed her with infinite care, as if breathing life into the lifeless puppet she had been, as if drawing the love they once had shared into painfully sweet reality again. "Invite me in, Paige." It was hardly more than a whisper, a distant echo of longing, but she obeyed. Stepping back, she waited as he closed the door, shutting them inside the house and into the memories. Without hesitation, her arms encircled his neck and invited his caress, even as her lips invited him to taste and savor the reunion, the surrender.

It felt like coming home, like returning to the familiar after being among strangers. Her world was here, in this house, in Jeff's arms. This moment wasn't one of surrender and it wasn't a reunion of lovers who had gone astray. It was renewal. It was springtime. It was music . . . a song for midnight . . . and she hadn't known how much she needed the melody of his lips on hers, the harmony of his breath, sweet and warm, against hers. She had missed him, but, somehow, those empty months faded into unimportance with the rhythm of their blending heartbeats.

His tongue brushed hers in tantalizing suggestion. His hands stroked the contours of her back, telling her in exquisite silence how well he remembered her secrets, how hard he had tried to forget. Paige nestled into his embrace and into the contentment and gentle happiness Jeff always had brought to her. There were no promises given, yet confidence flowed through her, yielding assurance to her hands as she touched him, imbuing her arms with strength to hold him close. She thought she probably had never been more vulnerable . . . or more unafraid.

If Jeff wondered at the eagerness of her response, he gave no sign. But as his kiss deepened with an intensity that left her weak with yearning, she knew he was as much a hostage of desire as she. This moment had been inevitable, as certain as the sunrise, and Paige gave freely, asking nothing more than to be allowed to love him, if only for the night.

Jeff forced his lips to release hers, but he couldn't

seem to establish any distance. Again and again he kissed her, lightly, teasingly, yet it was he who suffered, he who was torn between wanting and reason. He'd never wanted any woman—he'd never wanted *anything*—more desperately than he wanted Paige at this moment. How could he have been away from her, separated from her world for so long, and yet feel as if he were still such a part of her? What power did she possess to bring him again under her spell?

Even when he gained control, even when he pulled back, the soft trembling of her mouth lured him again. He didn't know how, after so many months apart, she could still evoke an aching tenderness from his heart. But he felt it stir, recognized its subtle insistence, and surrendered.

Gathering her close, he cupped a hand at the back of her head and held her against his chest. Her hair was satin, lustrous, and rich to the touch. He tangled his fingers into the strands, remembering the texture, thinking of the many times he had seen it splayed, silken dark, across his pillow. Paige fitted so perfectly against him. Her body shaped itself to his, matching curve to curve, pliant femininity to uncompromising masculine angles.

Every part of her was familiar to him, so why did he feel uncertain and hesitant? She apparently experienced no doubts about being in his arms. Her sigh of contentment had heightened his awareness of the risk he took in being near her, of the desire to give more of himself to her than she needed or wanted.

The sensation of simply holding her was making him think of quiet feelings he'd believed were dead and buried.

But they weren't. The fresh fragrance he inhaled with every breath reminded him of how very alive his senses really were, of how impossible it would be to pretend he didn't care. Paige moved against him, tracing the length of his arm with a restless fingertip, and he stopped fighting.

His lips found the hollow of her shoulder and he explored the pleasures hidden there. A shiver drifted through her. He felt it and tried to capture it with his embrace, but as her breasts pushed suggestively at his chest, Jeff gave his attention to capturing other, more provocative responses.

As his palm cradled her breast, Paige tightened her grip on him. It was purely self-defense. She knew if she relaxed so much as a finger, she would fall. Her legs felt too weak to be supporting her, so she assumed she stood only because Jeff held her. Closing her eyes, she admitted that the thought wasn't unsettling. Given the choice, she would probably stay like this forever. Or perhaps not *exactly* like this. . . .

"The bedroom . . . ?" Her throat closed around the words, making them a hoarse whisper, but she saw the look in his eyes, felt the tension ripple through him, and knew that he had heard.

"Paige . . ." His voice held a husky question, and for a heartstopping moment she thought he would deny his need and hers. But then his hand cupped her cheek and his thumb drew a mesmerizing circle at the corner of her mouth. One breathless second flowed into another. One heartbeat tripped into the next until her pulse was a quick, throbbing ache in her veins. His gaze dropped to her lips, returned to her eyes, and dropped again. Seduction murmured in the quiet, surrender trembled in the air, but Paige waited . . . waited until he spoke her name again.

"Paige." This time the question was gone, as was the hesitation. Gone. Replaced by decision and the confidence of the lover she remembered. He took her hand in his, and eagerness shimmered inside her as he led her down the hallway to the bedroom door. There he paused, turning her into his arms, pressing her back against the wall as he kissed her again.

The hunger caught her and she opened her mouth to the persuasive intrusion of his tongue. Still she wasn't close enough. Her fingers found a button on his shirt and worked it free until she could slip her hand inside.

Warm. He was so warm and rough and male. So familiar. So new. She had forgotten how good he felt to the touch. Oh, but she remembered the crisp, clean scent of him and the moist, seeking thrusts of his tongue and the hollow feeling centered low in her stomach. Desire seared her skin as she ran impatient fingertips across the hair texturing his chest. She neither knew nor cared how his shirt came loose, how it slipped away from his shoulders and fell to the floor. She only reveled in the sudden freedom to explore him not only with her hands, but also with dozens of tiny kisses.

He tasted a little salty and she smiled against his shoulder as she nuzzled a path along the tanned column of his throat. But the smile faded into a shaky sigh as Jeff pulled the neckline of her blouse down and away from her breasts. As he bent to sip and tantalize her, Paige arched into the caress, allowing the sensation, the heated expectancy, to engulf her. The feel of his palm stroking her bare spine was strong, slow enchantment. A trembling thrill raced through her, creating a melting fire deep inside.

She couldn't stand any more, couldn't wait any longer. Jeff, however, seemed to possess an indecent measure of patience. Even when she manipulated the buckle of his belt and unsnapped the stud of his jeans, he made no move toward the bed or satisfaction. He cooperated with her wishes, but only to the degree that it didn't interfere with his rediscovery of her.

From head to toe, he explored her, removing blouse, skirt, undergarments, any resistance she might have harbored. There was no escape, no reprieve from his searching hands or his demanding kisses. Not that she wanted deliverance. She couldn't imagine a sweeter prison than his arms. Her body, though, craved a more complete bondage, and with one convincing movement of her hand, she won a groan of consent from Jeff.

He lifted her and, despite the insistent kiss she

pressed to his mouth, he managed to carry her to the bed. Lowering her onto the mattress, he stood back and taunted her with the slow gaze that caressed her. Paige lay still, trying to achieve the casual nonchalance that seemed to come so easily for him. But when he placed his hands on the waistband of his jeans and pushed the denim past his hips and sinewy thighs, she saw and admired the proof of an impatience he couldn't hide.

Her arms opened with invitation. The curve of her lips was both timid and boldly seductive. She had shared this scene with Jeff before, each of them tempting the other, seeing who would give in to the desire first. But tonight Jeff made no concession to the games they had once played. His expression was somber, almost contemplative, as he bent his head to take her lips in a mute pledge that she couldn't interpret or understand.

There was no time then for anything except sensation—the pattern of passion he traced on her skin from chin to ankle, the texture of kisses that were warm and enticing, the rough-smooth touch of his flesh pressed to hers. She had made love with Jeff more times than she could recall, but she knew without reservation that he had never before been so skilled or so infinitely gentle.

Maybe it was the pain, all the soft hurts of loving, the forgiveness that had yet to be given, the forgetfulness that had yet to be gained. Paige wondered if Jeff was aware, as she was, of how transient these moments of happiness could be. It made his touch, his very presence beside her, a precious gift that she no longer had the privilege of taking for granted.

His possession was exquisite, a fulfillment for which she hadn't dared to hope. She held him close—as close as her strength would allow—while the passion flared like a shooting star in the depths of a midnight sky. And when it ebbed into lazy sparks of lingering desire, a tear slid from the corner of her eye, a tear that expressed in a wet, solitary trail all the wistful longings of her heart and the love that welled to overflowing in her soul.

She had changed the bedroom. He had no real objection to the redecorating, but somehow it bothered him out of all proportion that she hadn't left this room alone. Had she been so anxious to be rid of all reminders of his occupancy, of his place in her life?

In the night-shadowed room, Jeff tried to distinguish color and shape, just as his mind grappled with images of reality. Which was real? The contentment he felt as he lay in bed with Paige curled like a sleeping kitten beside him? Or the memory of her accusing eyes, her voice saying words that stripped away his trust in her? Hadn't he learned the hard way that love wasn't necessarily an emotion worthy of lofty praise and awe? It could be shallow and cheap, a feeling robbed of dignity.

A throaty sigh whispered against his skin, and his arm tightened reflexively across her shoulders. As she snuggled closer into the circle of his arm, her hair brushed his chin with velvety fragrance. Unbidden, his heart stumbled on an emotion he didn't want to recognize. What was he doing here, holding Paige like this, when he knew there was no future in it?

He ought to leave. Surely it would be easy this time. There was nothing to keep him. One night, a pleasant-enough interlude, didn't obligate him to stay. So why was he still beside her? Because, despite the changes in the room, despite the changes in him, he was home. Paige held him by the threads of a thousand memories and the complex tapestry of the life they had shared. Jeff closed his eyes. He didn't need to analyze or understand why he didn't move from the warm contentment of her bed. For the moment, it was enough to admit that regardless of all the good, sensible reasons for leaving, he simply wanted to stay.

When she stirred, he bent a reassuring caress to her forehead. She lifted her face to his, as if she were turning to him in the midst of a sweetly sensuous dream, and he let her draw him into the gentle seduction. In a matter of minutes, Jeff couldn't remember why he'd even considered leaving.

The doorbell shattered what should have been a peaceful awakening. Paige sat upright in bed, aware of the intrusion, unable to marshall her thoughts into complete consciousness. Beside her, Jeff moved restlessly and she smiled a welcome he didn't see. She remembered the night and her smile grew soft with the memory. Her hand moved toward the bronzed curve of his shoulder, carrying out her impulse to pull away the sheet and cover him with kisses.

But she paused, knowing in some still sleepy corner of her mind that something else called her attention. The doorbell. Pushing balky fingers through her hair, Paige wondered who . . . ? Her eyes settled lovingly on Jeff and she contemplated ignoring the ill manners of whoever was at her door. Even as the thought tempted her, she recalled why she had to get up and answer the door.

The bell chimed again as she left the bedroom and hurried down the hall, cinching the belt of her terrycloth robe as she walked. With a discontented yawn, she opened the door to her mother's sunny "Hello, dear. Did we wake you?"

Paige stifled a telling sigh and glanced past Mary's shoulder to Edward. He shrugged a cheerful apology. "You know how your mother is," he said affectionately. "She's been ready to leave on this trip since four o'clock this morning."

"It was five, Edward." Mary stepped forward into the house and Paige, of necessity, moved out of the way. "You know how he exaggerates, Paige."

Paige didn't care, but she tried not to show her impatience. "I'll get the quilt-top, Mother. I forgot you were coming by for it or I'd have had it ready." If she'd had any idea of just how inconvenient this early morning errand would prove, she'd have put the damn quilt on the porch. But Jeff had wiped all cohesive thoughts from her mind last night and. . . . Paige turned toward the bedroom, knowing she'd best save such reminiscing for later.

She'd almost reached the end of the hall before she realized Mary was following, still smiling, still chatting about the trip she and Edward were taking that day to visit Paige's grandmother in Arkansas. Paige stopped abruptly just short of the bedroom doorway. "Mother—"

"Are you sure you won't change your mind and come with us?" Mary stopped, too, and with motherly ease bent to pick up the discarded clothing which lay in careless testimony on the floor where Jeff had tossed them. "We'll be back tomorrow afternoon. Not too late, because you know Edward doesn't like to be away too long."

With a brisk flip of her wrist, Mary shook the wrinkles from Paige's skirt and smoothed it over her arm. "Honestly, Paige, just because you live by yourself" —she bent again, this time rescuing Jeff's shirt and giving it a shake—"there's no reason to throw your clothes all over the—" Her words and movements stopped in tandem as Mary held the shirt up, her gaze moving curiously from shoulder seam to shoulder seam.

Paige stepped in front of the doorway, hoping to block her mother's purposeful movement. There was a pregnant pause as Mary glanced past Paige's defensive stance into the bedroom. Wide green eyes mirrored a typically maternal worry for a split second before Mary's instinctive composure came to the fore. "Good morning, Jefferson. How nice to see you again."

A husky, incoherent response came from the bed, and Paige didn't know whether to bow her head in embarrassment or to let the utter absurdity of the situation wrap her in much-needed laughter. Fortunately, Mary removed the choice by thrusting the clothes into Paige's arms and stepping back with an undecided smile. "Put these away, dear, and get the quilt-top. I'll find Edward and we'll . . . wait outside."

"Mother," Paige tried to protest the hint of conspiracy in her mother's tone. She didn't intend to feel awkward, and if Mary thought there would be any discussion later, she would be disappointed. "It'll just take a second. There's no point in—"

"Nonsense," Mary said, lowering her voice a little bit, but not enough to keep Jeff from overhearing. "I'm just thankful the two of you have finally worked out your differences."

Mary turned and Paige was left standing in the doorway, feeling chastened and delinquent. How did her mother do it? she wondered. Not one word of disapproval had been spoken, yet . . .

"Get the quilt, Paige," Jeff ordered gruffly, "before she tells Edward and he decides to see this den of iniquity for himself."

An uncertain laugh caught in her throat as she

tossed an inquisitive glance at the bed. Jeff was sitting up, leaning against the headboard with the sheet draped loosely but adequately at his waist. "Don't worry," she said lightly, "I won't insist on a shotgun wedding." There was no answering amusement in Jeff's stormy expression, and Paige lifted her chin in defense. "It's none of their business anyway."

If anything, his frown darkened. "Then why do I feel as if we'd just gotten caught in the glare of the porchlight?"

"I can't imagine. It isn't bothering me."

His gaze dropped to her hands. "Oh, no—then what are you doing to my shirt?"

Paige frowned, realizing she was twisting the garment into a very tight ball. Dropping the shirt onto the foot of the bed, she shrugged. "I'll get the quilt-top. My grandmother is going to quilt it for me." A surreptitious glance told her Jeff wasn't interested in explanations or idle conversation. "I'll be back in a minute," she said as she took the quilt-top and started out the door.

Edward and Mary were in the entryway, heads bent in a quiet discussion that ended as Paige approached with a cautious but steady smile. There was a brooding look in the gaze her stepfather turned to her, a question that seemed to go beyond parental concern. She refused to let the awkwardness of the situation intimidate her. Handing her mother the quilt-top, Paige offered a nonchalant cheek for

Mary's good-bye. "Have a good trip," she said as her hand went to the doorknob.

"We will." Mary walked onto the porch and hesitated, waiting for Edward to follow. "You have a nice day too."

Paige nodded a reluctant acknowledgment of the wry comment. "I'll be fine, Mother."

Edward cleared his throat, seemed about to give some unsolicited advice, but then thought better of it. "Just be careful, Paige."

"I'll be fine," she repeated with perfect confidence as she began closing the door. With a last searching look, Edward stepped outside and Paige was able to shut out the two people who sometimes loved her a little too much. Sighing, she rested her forehead against the cool door. Now perhaps she could enjoy the morning and the delightful prospect of having Jeff to share it with her.

He was dressed when she entered the room and a healthy disappointment tugged at the corners of her mouth. "They're gone," she said unnecessarily. "I'm sorry. I knew they were supposed to stop by this morning, but I . . . well, I just forgot."

"Don't give it a thought."

At his tone, the letdown captured her lips completely. "What does that mean?"

He looked fully at her then, but his eyes were as dark and enigmatic as a moonless night. "Nothing."

It was the inflection of cool indifference that warned her of his anger. She didn't understand, couldn't think of a single reason for him to be upset, but she knew him too well to doubt it. The set of his shoulders and the tightness along his jaw would have told her even if he hadn't let the irritation slip into his voice.

"Where did I put my shoes?" he asked, and Paige bit her lip in indecision.

"I don't know. Did you have them on when we—?" She couldn't continue this banal intimacy and she saw no reason to ignore whatever was bothering him. Not talking had been one of the biggest problems in their marriage. "What's wrong, Jeff?"

He dropped to one knee and looked under the bed. "Here they are." Finding the shoes, he sat on the edge of the mattress to put them on. Paige intuitively moved to stand in front of him and placed her hands on his shoulders. When he looked up, she pressed a soft, persuasive kiss to his frown. His response was slow and not overly enthusiastic. With a sigh, she tried again. "Don't be upset. I'm not. It doesn't matter to me that Mother and Edward—"

"Paige, this isn't a good time to talk."

"Why?" A subtle irritation flashed through her and she brought her hands back to her sides. "Surely, after last night we can handle a little conversation."

His lips tightened, then relaxed with the breath he exhaled. "But especially *after last night* we can't handle an argument and that's what this little conversation is about to become." He bent his attention to his shoes again.

"I don't understand, Jeff." She tried to keep the uncertainty out of her voice but, with his heavy sigh, knew she hadn't succeeded.

He raised darkly impatient eyes to her face. "Paige, right now, I'm feeling guilty as hell. I'm not quite sure why I feel this way, but I know for damn sure that you and I have *not* worked out our differences. When I told you I had no interest in mending the tear in our marriage license, I meant it. One night together doesn't solve anything, and if you think—"

"I didn't make that statement! Mother did." Angrily, Paige crossed her arms and hugged her disappointment to her stomach. "Last night . . . happened. I wanted it. So did you. But I don't remember either one of us mentioning marriage, past or present. I haven't asked you for a commitment or an explanation of your reasons for coming here last night. I didn't even ask about your expectations or what, if anything, happens now. It isn't *my* fault that you feel guilty about being caught in bed with me. And frankly I resent your whole attitude." She paused for breath, which was a mistake.

Jeff rose, turning his height into advantage. "Well, I'm not crazy about your attitude either!" His hand raked through sleep-tousled hair. "Damn it, Paige. You see, we're arguing. Why didn't you just let it alone? I never could make you understand that occasionally silence is golden."

She couldn't believe it! "Are you trying to say that this stupid argument is *my* fault?"

"No, I'm saying—" He tipped his head back, stretching tense muscles in his neck and fighting a losing battle with his pride. "I don't know what in the hell I'm saying, Paige, and I can't tell you how I'm feeling. Last night was—good. More than good. Can we just leave it at that?"

She couldn't, he knew. Paige never had been able to give him space for thinking, time to come to grips with how *he* felt before sorting through her feelings. He watched her, waiting for another angry question, wishing he could simply take her in his arms and soothe the argument into oblivion.

"All right."

The quiet irritation in her reply caught him by surprise. He'd expected something more emphatic, less agreeable. Apparently, she really didn't want to fight. That bothered him more than his own ambiguity.

For as long as he'd known her, he and Paige had fought with each other because it was safer than soul-searching discussions. He thought he'd overcome that particular insecurity, that need to test her feelings by putting her on the defensive. But one night in her arms and one offhand comment by her mother and he was resorting to emotional games. What did he expect her to do? Admit she wanted him back? Did he want her to apologize over and over again for her lack of faith, the inadequacy of her love?

He turned from her, putting some distance between his confusion and the waiting expression in her blue eyes. "I'm leaving," he said evenly. "I suppose I'll see you on Monday."

It was a careless good-bye, and when she gave no response, he found he couldn't leave it at that. "Paige, look, I'm sorry I lost my temper. I wanted last night and this morning to be something special, but, well, it didn't work out that way. I can't seem to decide how I should feel about you and . . ." The apology would go no further and he could only hope she would understand. "I didn't mean for this to happen."

The curve of her lips was rueful. "I know, Jeff."

"I never should have come back."

"You don't mean that. It's important to put the past in perspective. Maybe for now we should just try to concentrate on who stole the NaeComp spec sheets and stop trying to explain why we spent the night together."

It didn't sound very satisfying to him, but then he'd backed himself into a corner and didn't seem to have much choice. "Good idea," he said with a tentative smile. "Any other inspirations?"

"Breakfast?"

A tender longing tugged at his heart. "Do you think we can handle that?"

"With ease," she assured him. "And we might even try a little conversation . . . just for fun."

"You can tell me how you came to make a quilt-top."

She walked to his side and slipped her hand into his as naturally as if there had never been a disagreeable word spoken. "You'll laugh."

"Probably, but not as much as you'll laugh when I tell you about my experience with hybrid tomatoes."

"Tomatoes?" Her startled question quickly dissolved into an uncertain laughter. "Oh, Jeff, don't tell me you've taken up gardening."

He straightened his shoulders with offended dignity, but the rueful grin gave him away. "Everything from radishes to zucchini."

"I'm impressed," she said, heroically trying to control her impulse to giggle. "I never knew you had an aptitude for growing vegetables."

"And I never knew that you knew which end of a needle to thread."

She squeezed his hand—hard—and led the way from the bedroom down the hallway to the kitchen. "Let's see if you remember how to make bacon omelets."

"Of course, I do. That's like riding a bicycle—once you learn how, you never forget."

A doubtful wrinkle creased her nose as she opened a kitchen drawer and pulled out a spatula. "All right, Mr. Lawrence. Start pedaling."

"Oh, no, you don't," he said as he took the utensil from her hand and waved it in front of her face. "This is an equal opportunity breakfast—no work, no food. Got it?"

She laughed, suddenly feeling more lighthearted than she had felt in a very long time. When she stood on tiptoe to press a teasing kiss on his chin, he smiled easily and the earlier tension faded into a comfortable camaraderie.

As the cooking progressed, the kitchen reflected the aura of happier days when they had shared breakfasts and conversations without giving a single thought to the wonder of simply enjoying each other's company. Paige listened to Jeff's stories about his gardening venture and she told him about her experience with arts and crafts.

He laughed often. So did she.

It was like the old times—the best of times.

CHAPTER SIX

In the days that followed, Paige daydreamed. Morning to night, no matter what she happened to be doing, Jeff was always in her thoughts. Her mood bounced between hope and uncertainty, never settling long in either state. She didn't like the new restlessness that kept her nervously waiting for something more to happen. It should have been enough to remember the night spent in his arms, the morning hours they'd shared before he'd left her with a kiss and a hesitant good-bye.

She knew Jeff wasn't ready to discuss the past and she knew there wasn't anything she could do about it . . . except wait. So she waited, watching for the smiles he sometimes gave her, wondering if the frown he often wore meant he was as unhappy with the indecision as she.

The week seemed a month long and when Saturday finally dawned again, Paige half expected him to call. She kept busy, but her heart jumped each time the phone rang. She didn't think he'd just drop by, but still she couldn't help looking out the window whenever she heard a car door slam. By Sunday she knew she had to talk to him, and from out of the blue her mind composed a surprisingly good excuse.

It wasn't until she reached his apartment building that she realized the idea was more than a reason to see him. Perhaps it had been on the fringes of her consciousness for a long time, waiting for her thoughts to turn toward the stolen papers. As she stood before the gray uniformity of his front door, she knew it was definitely something worth discussing with Jeff.

But when he opened the door, Paige hardly remembered her name, much less her reason for being there. She breathed a quiet "Hi," and wondered how she could suddenly feel so shy. It was incredible to experience the same adolescent butterflies, the jittery nervousness of her first encounter with romance. Of course, her first and only love had been Jefferson Lawrence. Maybe that explained the quiet pounding of her pulse and the erratic in-and-out rhythm of her breathing.

She didn't care. She only knew she ought to tell him her reason for disturbing his Sunday. But how could she think when he looked so invitingly relaxed, so ruggedly disheveled? And though it hadn't reached his lips, there was a smile nestled deep in the autumn darkness of his eyes—a smile that made her feel warm and welcome and wanted.

"Hello, Paige." He held the door wide. "Come in. I was just thinking about you."

Pleasure tingled all the way to her toes. "You were? Really?"

As her lips curved in an expression he remembered so very well, Jeff wondered why he'd spent the entire week denying that he wanted to be with her. "I was. Really," he said softly, and then didn't know if he should tell her what he'd been thinking or if he just should kiss her and let her draw her own conclusions. Somehow, though, he couldn't quite find the courage to do either and he opted for a lighter touch. "I was wishing I had someone to help me clean this place."

As suddenly as it had come, her shyness disappeared. It could have been his teasing, or the amusement tucked at the corner of his mouth. Or, she supposed, it could be her own need to share the idea about the spec sheets. The sooner that riddle in their past was solved, the sooner they could begin resolving their personal lives.

She stepped inside the apartment and frowned at the clutter. "Try the classified ads, Jeff. There are plenty of reputable cleaning services listed in the Sunday paper."

"Do you think they have an emergency crew for weekends?"

Paige cleared papers from the sofa so she could sit down. "I doubt it. Short of declaring this apartment a disaster area and calling in the National Guard, I think you're on your own."

"Except for you." His smile disarmed her resistance. "Is there any chance you could be persuaded . . . ?"

"Maybe . . . for a soda." She tried to sound as doubtful as possible. "At least I'll let you convince me I ought to keep you company. And if you throw in a snack, I might even let you in on an idea that just occurred to me."

"Must be a hell of an idea if you're willing to sell it for a few potato chips."

"Is that all you're going to offer?"

He lifted a suggestive brow. "From the kitchen, yes. The cupboards are pretty bare. But there are other—"

"Forget the chips and the soda. You can take me out for dinner later."

He sank onto the sofa cushion beside her, not bothering to move the sheets of paper scattered there and shuffling the clutter by propping his feet on the coffee table. "Can't. I have to work." With a gesture of his hand, he indicated the obvious. "Believe it or not, there is method to this madness."

"Could you prove that?" She was painfully conscious of his long, muscular body so very close to her and her voice grew husky with the awareness.

"Not according to Toby. He's been complaining that the work load at our consulting firm is more than he can handle and so he mailed some of the paperwork to me. I haven't been able to convince him that I'm not on an extended vacation."

"Hmmm." Paige would have liked to question him

about his business associate and about the business. But a holdover pride kept her silent. "Aren't you curious about my idea?" she asked instead.

"Mmm-hmm." He leaned his head against the cushion and closed his eyes, a perfect picture of intense *in*curiosity.

Paige thought she demonstrated tremendous control by keeping her elbow tucked close to her side instead of letting it rattle a couple of his ribs. "It would serve you right if I didn't tell you."

"I'm listening, Paige," he said, but his eyes remained closed, his expression relaxed and sleepy. "You can hold out for a better offer if you want, but potato chips and pop is the best I can do."

"Then I suppose I'll accept, because there isn't anyone else around to tell." She paused to run a fidgety palm over her denim-clad thigh. "I've been trying to recreate the circumstances surrounding the theft, and this afternoon, all of a sudden, it occurred to me that the spec sheets could have been taken from the folder *before* it was returned to security."

Jeff's sigh was slow and weary. "Paige, the NaeComp spec sheets and folder were in the boardroom from one-thirty until three o'clock on Friday before they were discovered missing the following Monday. I attended that meeting and I returned the NaeComp folder, plus two other files, to security afterward."

"Did you look inside the folders at all?"

"Not that I recall." He sighed. "But all three files were opened at some point during the meeting."

"But did you actually *see* the project specification sheets?"

"Yes." His fingers raked transient waves through his toasty hair, but his eyes opened. "At least, I think I saw them."

She waited, hoping the details of that day would return to his memory.

"I'm sure they were inside the folder, Paige. Mitch and Sandi both made reports on that contract. Then there was some discussion about the delay in the production schedule—I clearly remember that as being a waste of time. Edward ordered the delay so Sandi could make a separate cost analysis, which ended up being just a duplication of a report I'd already done."

"Did Sandi and Mitch use the spec sheets during their presentations?"

Jeff slid her a rueful glance. "You missed your calling, Paige. You were born to be a D.A."

This time her elbow did make contact, but lightly, teasingly, and her arm stayed close to his. "Objection overruled, Mr. Lawrence. Answer the question."

"I wish I could, but I honestly don't remember. I've been in dozens of similar meetings, looked at dozens of files and spec sheets and production reports. And for that particular Friday, all I would swear to is that Edward gave the folder to me at the end of the meeting and I took it to the vault."

Paige pursed her lips and traced a fingertip pattern on the sofa arm. "Could Sandi or Mitch have used the specs and then not put them back in the folder?"

"In front of everyone?" Jeff laughed a mirthless disbelief. "That would have been a damn risky thing to do."

"Maybe not, Jeff. It would have been so unlikely, who would have thought to question some shuffling of papers? And even if someone had noticed, it could have been laughed off as an honest mistake." She paused to mull the possibilities. "If we go on that assumption, then Sandi and Mitch would be the prime suspects. I can believe that Mitchell Brewer would do anything for money, but I have trouble believing he could be so clever. And Sandi . . . I don't have any idea why she would steal—"

"From you?" Jeff straightened and brought one foot to the floor as he turned to face Paige. "Did I imagine this, or was there really some gossip a few years ago about an affair between Sandi and Gary Glendenning?"

"It wasn't just gossip. Gary told me they were pretty serious for a while, but he broke it off quite some time ago."

"And came back to you?"

"That doesn't deserve an answer, Jeff. You know how I feel about Gary."

"And I know how he feels about you, which is something I'm sure Sandi is well aware of too. And didn't Gary's company pick up several of Randall

Electronics' contracts after the security leak was discovered?"

"We certainly lost several contracts, but whether or not Gary was able to profit from our loss, I couldn't say. Gary is so fiercely independent and close-mouthed about his electronics business. He just doesn't discuss it with me or anyone else."

"That Ferrari he drives shows that he's obviously improved his financial situation in the past couple of years. Maybe Sandi has been selling information to support his sports car habit. That way she keeps Gary obligated to her and hurts your company at the same time."

"Randall Electronics wasn't actually *hurt* by the losses. We've been in business a long time and almost all of our customers remained loyal. Besides, Gary told me he and Sandi weren't seeing each other anymore." Paige noticed the skeptical arching of Jeff's eyebrows. "He wouldn't lie to me."

"Don't be naive, Paige."

She moved her arm away from his. "Don't be irritating, Jeff."

"It's my apartment." He paused and a slow smile mellowed the stubborn line of his jaw. "No, this is really your apartment, isn't it? All right, then, I won't start an argument, but you probably ought to avoid talking about your cowboy."

"Maybe *you* should avoid talking about *your* blonde."

He grinned. "Sandi? Is she blonde? Funny, I hadn't

noticed. She has other . . . more interesting attributes."

"Jefferson Lawrence, you're—" Paige caught her protest as his amusement became a lazy laugh. "You haven't changed a bit."

Instantly, the mood changed. The teasing look, the friendly ambience gave way to sobering memories. "Oh, yes, I have," he said. "I've changed more than I care to admit. My life isn't perfect now, Paige, but I like it a lot."

Her heart felt suddenly tight and uncomfortable. "Your life in Oklahoma City." She hated to add the qualification, but it seemed necessary: "Your life . . . without me."

The huskiness in her voice, her unnatural stillness, brought a knot of regret to his throat and for long, painful seconds he couldn't speak. "It isn't exactly what I had planned, Paige."

A rueful sigh slid slowly from her lips. "I guess it's true that 'life happens to you while you're making other plans.' But I don't understand what happened to us, Jeff. For two years I've tried to piece it all together, to remember why we were so angry, to see why you left and how I let you."

"Did you think if you offered me the Tri-Star project and brought me back into your life temporarily that I would give you the answers?"

"I hoped we might be able to talk about it, maybe clear up a few misunderstandings."

Jeff felt her hesitancy, but he didn't know how to

reassure her; wasn't sure he wanted to try. "What do you think that will accomplish?"

Paige turned a level, if slightly wounded, gaze to his face. "Maybe nothing. But at least I'll know."

So would he. And that, Jeff realized, was the source of his own reluctance. He wasn't at all sure he wanted to know. "Where would we even begin, Paige? With the argument we had about waiting until you finished college before getting married? You won that one and never graduated. Should we skip to the argument we had about buying a house? Or maybe we should talk about all the times you were mad because I worked late on a project. After all, Randall Electronics was *your* company and no one was going to fire me."

"I didn't realize you resented my position in the company."

"Not *your* position, Paige, but the way you continually reminded me of mine."

She caught the impulse to deny it. "You might have told me before, Jeff. I never meant to. . . ."

"I know you didn't. Maybe that's why I found it so hard to say anything. It would only have ended in an argument, anyway."

He was right, she knew. Her temper was every bit as quick as his, but just as quickly diffused. "I never felt threatened by the fact that we argued, Jeff. Did you?"

"No, I accepted that as part of our relationship. I even enjoyed disagreeing with you at times. And you know I couldn't stay angry with you for very long." He glanced at her bent head, at the dark, glossy hair that shielded her expression from him. Then he stared at a framed print on the far wall. "No, Paige, I never felt threatened by our arguments. At least, not until . . ."

His voice went quiet with memory and, beside him, Paige didn't have to ask what he was remembering. She knew. Two years hadn't dimmed her ability to recall that long-ago day. . . .

It had been an uneventful Friday for her. She'd made plans for the evening. Nothing elaborate, just she and Jeff meeting a few friends at a favorite restaurant for dinner. He surely would have no objections about that, or so she'd thought.

But it had been a long and tiring Friday for Jeff and he'd made some plans of his own. It was high time, he had thought, that he and Paige made a definite decision about the future. He was tired of working for Randall Electronics, weary of proving that being married to the owner of the company had nothing to do with his ability as an engineer. He was ready to move away from Tulsa, from the friends that Paige kept constantly underfoot, from the pressures that were building in their marriage. Surely, she would understand how important this new business venture was to him.

She hadn't understood. She hadn't even wanted to discuss it. The argument had been quick and lethal. He'd issued an ultimatum in anger and she had answered in anger. Paige could still hear the door slamming behind him; she could still recall the frantic pounding in her head and the sudden, insidious beginning of fear.

The framed print came into focus once again and the silence in the apartment grew oppressive. Impulsively, Jeff reached for her hand and held it cradled between his palms. "I never intended to leave you forever, Paige. That Friday night, when we quarreled, I only wanted to give us both some time to cool off, to think. I knew if I didn't do something to change the situation, it was going to get even worse. So I went back to the office, typed out a letter of resignation, and took everything personal from my desk. Then I drove to Oklahoma City and spent the weekend with Toby, making plans for the new business and wondering what I was going to say to you when I got back." His fingers pressed against hers in mute appeal. "If I'd had any idea how incriminating my actions would appear on Monday morning when the theft of those spec sheets was discovered—"

"And if I'd known what was going to happen to us—" Her voice broke. She couldn't even think about that awful morning without getting cold chills. That lost weekend had been bad enough—she'd spent her time alternating between justifying her anger with Jeff and admitting she was a spoiled, stubborn idiot who didn't deserve his love. Finally, she had realized she was going to have to make some concessions. She didn't understand or share his obsession to open a computer consultation service, but if it meant so much to him, she supposed she could adjust. When she still hadn't heard from him on Sunday night, she decided she could adjust to anything if only he'd come home.

It hadn't been worry that had kept her pacing the floor that night—she'd felt certain she knew where Jeff had gone and why. When he'd first broached the subject of opening his own firm, he had mentioned a college friend, Toby Welch, as a possible business partner. Paige hadn't asked too many questions. The idea that Jeff wasn't happy with the life she'd tried to create for him had bothered her immensely and she'd been reticent to discuss plans that didn't seem to require any input from her. But knowing where he was didn't ease the fear that a change in her life was imminent.

It wasn't until much later—when it no longer mattered—that she learned of the circumstances that had delayed Jeff's return: the decision to stay another night, just long enough to look at a possible office site, then the delay caused by a traffic accident on the turnpike. It had been almost noon Monday before Jeff had walked into Edward's office and faced the suspicious looks and thinly veiled indictment of his weekend activities.

Paige shivered as the scene ran through her mind for probably the thousandth time. "Jeff, I never believed even for a second that you had anything to do with the theft. But Edward kept asking me over and over again where you were, when you were coming back, why you'd decided to resign without talking to him, what you planned to do. He tried not to let me see how worried he was, but Mitch wouldn't allow anyone time to think. He kept stirring the questions, pointing out that there was only one executive board member missing—you. When he said it was obvious you'd stolen the specs, I couldn't stand any more. I lied to protect you, Jeff. I created an alibi for you—a story to cover your actions. I didn't know what else to do. I told them—"

"It doesn't matter, Paige." He didn't know how he kept from choking on the words. It did matter, but he couldn't bear to hear her explanation again. If she'd really believed in his innocence, she would have seen no need for an alibi. That absence of trust, the realization that Paige—who supposedly loved him more than anyone else in the world—had lied instead of letting the truth stand against the evidence was devastating.

He could have coped with the questions; he could have answered the implication of guilt with honesty. But when faced with the choice of either defending his integrity or revealing Paige's utter lack of faith in him, he suddenly had discovered he no longer cared what anyone thought.

Restless now, he pulled his gaze from the picture and stood, shrugging aside the memory and the hurt that refused to heal. "It doesn't matter, Paige," he repeated. "Maybe we're just beating our heads against the wall in thinking that finding the real thief will make any difference. Maybe we should have left well enough alone."

Well enough? Was that how he described a life without her in it? "What we *should* have done," she corrected firmly, "was face the accusations then. And we should have talked far more than we did before deciding to divorce."

Jeff rubbed the tension at the back of his neck. "I told you once, Paige, we never learned the art of communication. We only knew the art of arguing."

"That isn't entirely true, Jeff. I think we were just afraid to be really honest with each other."

He turned to look at her. Sincerity sparkled azure-soft in her eyes, her lips curved in a gentle wish, her hair formed a silken shadow around her face. Jeff thought she had never been more beautiful. He wished he could pretend the past two years had never happened. He wished he could make love to her now and forget that their relationship had ever been less than perfect. But wishes, like hindsight, had little to do with reality.

"So what happens now, Paige? Where do we go from here?"

It was an unfair question and she didn't have an answer. Frustration burrowed deep inside her. What did he expect her to say? "I could ask you the same thing, Jeff."

"And if you did, I suppose I'd have to say I don't know. I had no intention of getting involved with you again, Paige." He paused, walked back to the sofa, and stood in pensive silence. "But then I had no intention of getting a divorce either."

"We were too angry, too upset to make that decision." In her mind, even now, she could hear the awful things they had said to each other. After the scene in Edward's office, Jeff had left and she had followed him home. Then she had followed him from room to room as he packed his things; she had listened to the accusations he'd hurled at her and she had responded in kind.

But the emotion that had shrouded their words was unlike anything Paige had ever experienced. Her anger had been produced by confusion and fear, but Jeff's . . . She hadn't understood his reasons for leaving; hadn't been able to comprehend that he *was* leaving her. When she'd asked what he wanted from her, he'd turned a cold, uncaring face to her and suggested a divorce. A quiet, furious indifference had been her only recourse and she'd replied heatedly that if a divorce was what he wanted, that was what he would get.

Now, looking up at him, knowing how much she cared, Paige didn't know how she could have flung such hateful words at him, how she could have allowed their marriage to end in a few moments of careless anger. But he'd left, and a part of her had died.

"Maybe life is giving us a second chance, Jeff."

His half smile offered no promises. "I suppose only time will tell."

At least he hadn't denied the possibility, she thought as she stood to face him. For a provocative moment, they exchanged a quiet look, a hesitant understanding. Then Paige went on tiptoe to bestow a light kiss on his cheek. "Since it's obvious you're not going to come through with the potato chips and soft drink, I'm going to leave you to your method of madness."

His arm circled her waist as if it belonged there, but she sensed that his heart was at war with his logic. "I'm glad you came. I wish you could stay."

She wished so, too, but she thought he needed some time alone to absorb the fact that they had actually talked about the past without arguing and without anger. She could use a little time to think about that herself. "Let me know when you get this place cleaned up and the refrigerator restocked and I'll come back."

"You want to reap the benefits without doing any of the work, is that it?"

She smiled, feeling happier than she had in weeks. "That's it."

She wasn't surprised at the gentle good-bye he pressed to her lips, and although she was tempted, she didn't linger in his arms. There would be another time for that, she told herself as she walked through the Sunday afternoon sunshine to her car. If she had anything at all to say about it, there would be an abundance of time to spend loving Jeff.

Across the street, hidden in the shadow of an overgrown elm, an engine idled as long, narrow fingers tapped a leather-covered steering wheel. As Paige drove away from the apartment complex, a meditative gaze turned toward Jeff's door.

She'd been with him again. A reconciliation attempt was the obvious explanation, of course. But still, there had been questions asked lately. Pointed questions. About Gary. About Gary's company. And Lawrence wasn't the type to let well enough alone.

The fingers gripped the wheel in reluctant decision. *Something would have to be done. There just wasn't any other choice.*

The car responded to command and pulled slowly from the shade of the elm to merge with the lazy flow of Sunday afternoon traffic.

CHAPTER SEVEN

"Paige, could I see you in my office, please?" Without waiting for her reply, Jeff replaced the telephone receiver and impatiently drummed his fingers on the desk top.

He couldn't ignore the warning this time. He should have realized what was happening sooner. But it had been so subtle: a few misplaced papers, a couple of files out of order in the file cabinet, nothing that couldn't be explained away as a trick of memory. Until this.

Pushing away from the desk, he rose to give himself room to think. For the first time in weeks, he wished for the comfort and space of his office in Oklahoma City. That was his home now, his corner of the world, and yet in so many ways Tulsa was home to him as well. Coming back had been like putting on an old pair of shoes and discovering a familiar fit.

Jeff didn't doubt that with only minor adjustments he could fit back into the life he'd known here before. And he didn't doubt that Paige hoped he would choose to do so. But he wouldn't. Too much had happened. He'd invested too much of himself in making a new life away from the past, away from the hurt. If there was any fitting in to be done, Paige would have to be the one to do it. He wasn't sure she would and hadn't quite reached the point of admitting he wanted her to.

Jeff frowned and rubbed the strain from his forehead. It was a little frightening to think that despite all the reasons he shouldn't, he still cared.

"Jeff?"

Paige's voice, concerned and low, filtered into his train of thought. He turned to face her and his heart pounded unsteadily against his ribs. How long could he deny the emotion that knotted his stomach whenever he saw her? And why, when her lack of trust had caused him so much heartache, did he automatically turn to her, trusting her, seeking her help? He didn't know, but he recognized the relief flowing through him just because she was near.

"Take a look at this." He tapped the folder on his desk and watched as she moved to obey.

She barely glanced at the identification tab before opening the folder and leafing through the papers inside. Jeff tensed when she paused, her fingers sliding along the edge of several stapled sheets as her forehead wrinkled in puzzled thought. The realization of what she held dawned slowly and she lifted her eyes to his in uncertain question.

"This is a classified report," she said in a hushed

and breathy whisper. "The projected costs and proposed bid for the Clemons contract."

He nodded and walked around the desk to close the door. "There must be at least half a dozen electronics firms that would love to have that contract."

"This information would certainly come in handy in bidding against us, wouldn't it?" Paige drew a long, unsteady breath. Her gaze went again to the papers as question after question tumbled through her mind, but she couldn't decide which one to tackle first. She knew there was one answer, one single thread of logic, that tied everything together, but it eluded her grasp and tangled with a host of unsettling feelings. "Who could have done this, Jeff? And why?"

Until that moment, he hadn't realized he was holding himself under such strict control; hadn't acknowledged the fear that she might look at him with suspicion. He released his breath slowly. "It's a warning, Paige. Whoever slipped that report into the Tri-Star folder on my desk didn't intend for me to be caught with it. If that had been the object, the papers wouldn't have been placed where I'd be bound to find them first thing this morning. They were put here to show me how easily I could be indicted again."

"So I guess we're getting close to discovering. . . ." She didn't finish the sentence, but in the silence there was the shared knowledge that suspicions and conjecture now were something more. Almost hesitantly she flipped the top sheets aside to find the signature on the report. "Mitch," she said softly, not really surprised and yet not entirely accepting either. "I guess he—"

"We can't jump to that conclusion, Paige, no matter how logical it might seem. There are other employees who have access to this information."

"But how could this happen with the strict security measures we use? Not just anyone can enter the vault. There's a security guard and a logbook record of all the activity during the day. How could someone simply walk out with this report?" She tapped the pages against the desk for emphasis, feeling suddenly angry that such a thing could happen in *her* company.

"Paige, whoever has done this is your employee. A trusted and valued employee. A friend. Someone you have worked with for a very long time. Someone you'd swear could have no reason to steal from Randall Electronics."

She knew that, of course. She just hadn't wanted to accept the disappointment that had to come. It was so much easier to keep a buffer zone of doubt and disbelief between herself and the moment she would have to face putting a name to that "someone." With a sigh, she dropped the report on the desk. "Do you think it's Mitch?"

"I don't know yet. Everything I've found out about his life-style during the past couple of years lends itself to a motive. Mitchell Brewer lives very comfortably for a man who earns the salary he does. But maybe he's made some sound financial investments." Jeff shrugged at the possibility. "I don't think we can rule out Sandi, either. Mitch may have compiled the report, but she has equal access to the information."

"Her life-style doesn't suggest much comfort, though."

"Sandi wouldn't take this kind of risk only for profit. If she's involved, then so is Gary Glendenning."

Paige lifted her chin to challenge the idea. "You can't honestly believe Gary is involved in stealing from Randall Electronics. He may not have a great deal of affection for his father, but he respects Edward enough not to steal from him. And that's what it would amount to. Edward doesn't own this company, but he's invested a lot of himself in it over the years." She shook her head, affirming her original conviction. "I just can't see how Gary could be a part of this. Besides, why would Sandi take all the risks if Gary reaped all the benefits?"

Jeff didn't believe for one minute that Sandi was that selfless, but he wasn't about to accept Paige's glowing faith in that grinning cowboy either. He didn't have an answer and he wasn't ready to point the finger of accusation yet. In his mind, Mitch, Gary, and Sandi were all suspects, and until he had evidence against one in particular, he couldn't eliminate the other two. He stroked his thumb along the pensive line of his jaw. "Well, whoever is responsible went to the trouble of trying to warn us, so we must be on the right track."

"What should we do now?"

The upward tilt of his lips were humorless. "I guess I'll ask Sandi out to dinner again and try to probe the secrets of her passion for cowboys. Then I suppose I'll make a point of asking Brewer about the stock market."

Paige nodded her understanding and smiled as she offered to help. "I'll talk to Gary and see what I can find out about his business. He doesn't usually like to discuss it, but maybe—"

"Be careful what you say to him, Paige," Jeff interrupted. "I know you don't believe he knows anything about the theft, but I'm not so sure. So just play it safe. All right?"

"Right." She gave him a snappy salute, feeling suddenly eager to reach the end of the puzzle and the end of the tension. The sooner the truth was known, the sooner she and Jeff could settle the unsettled question that lay between them. "Safe and sensible," she said. "And don't worry about a thing, Jeff. You have no reason to be jealous."

With a coy toss of dusky hair, she started for the door, only to turn back and retrieve the stapled report from his desk. Her smile as well as her mood sobered a little when she met his eyes. "I'll make sure this is taken care of."

She hesitated, but Jeff couldn't voice the approval he knew she waited for. He would have preferred to handle matters on his own. But the simple truth was that he needed her help.

When she left his office, he ignored the work awaiting his attention and stared out the rectangular window for a long time. *No reason to be jealous,* she'd said.

It wouldn't—necessarily—have occurred to him to worry about Paige spending time with Gary. And as to being jealous, well, Jeff thought he'd come to grips with that emotion. However, he couldn't stop wondering how, exactly, Paige planned to elicit information from that overly amorous cowboy.

Jeff warned his imagination to be sensible. He wasn't jealous. He had no reason to be. She'd just told him so.

Still, she'd seemed very eager to keep an eye on Gary.

Around and around his thoughts whirled, making him aware that he was being unfair, not only to her, but to himself as well. With each passing day, it became more apparent to him that his life—no matter how good he'd convinced himself it was—wasn't complete without Paige. He wanted to have the right to feel protective toward her, to feel confident her teasing was simply teasing.

Maybe he was expecting too much of her. She had changed in subtle ways and he believed she truly wanted to resolve their past problems and have that second chance she'd mentioned. He'd noticed how she made an effort to consider his feelings now, where before she'd always been so sure her way was best for both of them.

Jeff frowned at the rectangle of sunlight. That wasn't fair either, he thought. There had been times when he'd been every bit as stubborn as she. During the last year of their marriage, he'd argued the case for independence more times than he could recall. He'd gone so far as to demand that she leave everything—her job, family, home, and friends—so he could have what he wanted: his own business.

He was willing to accept half of the responsibility for the divorce, but before he would make any move toward a second chance Jeff knew he'd have to give the future some heavy thought. Regardless of the pressures that had cracked the foundation of their marriage, Paige had delivered the final, fatal blow.

For two years he'd lived with the belief that she had done something unforgivable by not having a strong, unshakable faith in his integrity. Maybe, though, he'd been wrong to assume that love automatically meant trust. Maybe trust had to be nurtured, just as all aspects of a relationship had to develop and grow. Maybe it was time he considered forgiving and forgetting.

The telephone rang, interrupting his thoughts and redirecting his attention to the day's work.

It was late, long after five o'clock, before Jeff leaned back in his chair and stretched the day's tension from his muscles. There was an absence of noise in the office and, in the hallway beyond his door, he sensed the emptiness in the building. Funny, he thought, he hadn't been aware of the passing of time or the sounds of departing workers. Too many things on his mind, perhaps. Or possibly too absorbed in wrapping up his part of the Tri-Star project. A few more days, no more than two weeks at most, and his job for Randall Electronics would be finished. He only hoped he'd be able to tie up the other loose ends by that time as well.

With a slow smile, Jeff wondered how Paige would feel about being called a loose end in his life. He didn't have a chance to ruminate on the possibilities, though, before the telephone on his desk interrupted.

"Lawrence." He cradled the receiver against his shoulder as he answered and busied his hands in straightening the papers on his desk.

Silence was the only answer and after a moment, a definitive click. Frowning, Jeff returned the receiver to the base. Anyone who answered the telephone after working hours deserved that response, he decided. After closing time, it was almost bound to be a wrong number.

He spent a few minutes putting files away and deciding what would require his attention on Monday morning. Then he gathered together the few letters intended for the mailroom. As he picked up a large brown envelope, already addressed, stamped, and sealed, he thought that whatever complaints he might have about this office, he couldn't find fault with the efficiency of the secretarial staff.

Reaching for a pen, he added a bold "Attn: Ken Brown" to the bottom left corner of the envelope. Then he placed it with the other outgoing mail. Ken would be pleased to receive the analysis on the computer malfunction earlier than promised and Toby would be happy that Jeff had done the report. All in all, including the amount of work he'd completed on Tri-Star, Jeff thought he'd accomplished a great deal for one day. It felt good to switch out the light, knowing he wasn't leaving a mountain of work behind.

When he reached his car, Jeff unlocked the door and wondered if he should try to phone Sandi when he reached his apartment or if he could put off that dubious pleasure until later. He started to get into the car, but a light in a narrow, rectangular window caught his eye and he paused.

That was his office. Quickly, he scanned the back of the building, counting windows to confirm the location. But even as he did, the light went out again. *Odd,* he thought. Why would anyone be in his office now? His first impulse was to go back, but he wasn't sure what that would accomplish. Whoever had been there would be gone before he could even get inside the building. And he supposed the light could have been flipped on by accident—by someone, although he couldn't imagine who.

Jeff patted the top of the car as he considered the possibilities. There could be any number of legitimate explanations, but he had a gut feeling that none of them applied. In sudden decision, he got into the car, started the motor, and drove away from Randall Electronics. At the end of the drive, he turned onto the highway and drove a short distance before pulling to the side of the road. He parked in the shadowed space between two tall pecan trees and settled back to wait. Whoever had been in his office would have to pass this way sooner or later and Jeff intended to see who it might be.

The first time he squinted at his wristwatch through the gathering dusk, he felt a little foolish. Ten minutes later when he checked the time again, he decided he was not cut out for surveillance work. Just as he was about to admit he was wasting a perfectly good Friday evening, a car turned onto the highway from the company road.

Jeff watched as it drove past, noting the shiny luxury of Edward Glendenning's Chrysler. *Nice car,* Jeff thought. Edward might be able to tell him who else had been in the building tonight. Turning his gaze to the intersection behind him, Jeff decided that if his detective work didn't net any conclusions, he'd ask Edward about the names on the company's overtime list.

He had to wait no more than a few minutes, though, before a second car made the turn onto the highway. As it passed, he recognized the crumpled fender of Sandi Winners's Mustang convertible. He pursed his lips as the sporty coupé faded from his view. So Sandy had been working late. He tried to remember if she made a habit of it, but he'd never been interested enough to ask.

A squeal of tires echoed through the stillness and Jeff turned his head just in time to watch a small foreign job streak past. Mitchell Brewer, Jeff thought. His hell-for-leather driving style was as distinctive as Sandi's crumpled fender any day.

With a heavy frown, Jeff turned the key in the ignition and eased his car onto the highway once again. He didn't know what he'd achieved by sitting in the dark watching the traffic. Sandi and Mitch both had been in the building late, so he still had to decide which of them might be guilty. It wasn't a question he could resolve tonight. He didn't have any desire to reason through the day's events now, anyway. A quiet evening, a good night's sleep, would clear his mind for that kind of analytical thought.

Now, if only he could reason away the nagging worry about what Paige might be doing with Gary Glendenning . . .

When he reached the apartment complex, Paige was waiting outside his door and Jeff tried not to show his relief or the pleasure rippling through him. "Don't tell me your cowboy turned you down?" he said in a teasing tone.

"All right, I won't tell you." She crossed her arms and leaned against the window as she waited for him to unlock the door. "As long as you'll admit you didn't have any better luck with Sandi."

He raised his hands in surrender. "I admit it. Would you like to come in and console me?"

She shrugged a saucy indifference. "I wouldn't want to appear easy, but you know I'll do almost anything for some Chinese food."

"I don't have any on hand."

"But you're going to go out and get some while I put a few records on the stereo, aren't you?"

His brows arched in surprise as he pushed open the door and motioned her inside. "For a woman who doesn't want to appear easy, you seem to have made quite a few plans for my evening."

Her lips curved in seductive mystery. "Any objections?"

"Only to going out again. Frankly, I'm not hungry for Chinese food."

"But you'd get some for me, wouldn't you?"

At that moment, Jeff thought he would have done almost anything she asked. He followed her into the apartment and closed the door. "That depends on what else you have planned for tonight."

She clasped her hands and dropped her gaze in demure fashion. "I think you'll like what I have in mind. After dinner, I thought we might sit on the sofa, listen to music, and . . ."

"So far, so good," he prompted.

"Then I thought you'd like for me to"—she lifted

mischievous eyes to his—"tell you what I did with the Clemons report."

"I knew this was beginning to sound too good to be true."

"Don't you want to know?"

"Is there a choice?"

Hands at her hips, Paige gave him a frown. "Jefferson Lawrence, you have an astonishing lack of curiosity."

He took off his suit jacket and tossed it across the back of a chair. "That comes from too much amateur sleuthing. I have new respect for private investigators. Television makes it look far too easy."

"What kind of sleuthing have you been doing?"

A soft humor tugged at the corner of his mouth as he loosened the knot of his tie. "I've been finding out what a tough life the average policeman has. Sitting on the side of the road with a radar gun for company can't be all that exciting, you know."

"Jeff. . . ." Paige was thoroughly confused. "Did you, uh, stop for something to drink after work?"

He laughed and sank onto the sofa. As he unlaced his shoes, he told her about seeing the light in the office window. By the time he'd finished the recital of his evening surveillance, Paige, too, had discarded her shoes and was sitting next to him.

"What do you suppose he was looking for in your office?" she asked.

"Well, assuming that he—or she—*was* responsible

for the light I saw, I'd guess the purpose was to find the Clemons report."

"Surely, no one would think you'd keep it, Jeff. The obvious thing to do would be to get rid of it immediately . . . or turn it over to Edward."

"Mitch and Sandi are both aware of the strain between your stepfather and me. I don't think either one of them would believe I'd confide in Edward . . . no matter how obvious. Eventually, someone is going to decide you're helping me."

"Well, there's no way that report can be traced to you. I destroyed it after checking the file in security this afternoon. The original report was right where it was supposed to be, so the papers you found were copied. Mitch must have duplicated the information before submitting the original report."

"It certainly looks that way, but I don't know, Paige. Mitch is so openly antagonistic, so quick to defend the integrity of Randall Electronics. He worked long and hard to regain the contracts that were lost after the security leak two years ago. He could be clever enough to hide behind an outward loyalty, but—" Jeff paused, and absently, it seemed, his arm went around Paige's shoulders. "Something just doesn't feel right about this whole thing, but I can't figure out what it is."

"We might have to discuss this with Edward." Paige sensed Jeff's negative opinion and she took his hand in hers. "I know he hasn't made you feel very welcome, but he's only being protective of me, Jeff.

He knows, probably more than anyone else, how much I was hurt when you left. I'm not sure I could have survived without his and Mother's support."

Jeff stood abruptly and walked to the stereo. His movements were crisp and controlled as he sorted through a stack of records. Paige sighed softly, knowing what he was thinking, feeling, as if she could read his mind. *He'd* been hurt, too, and he'd survived on the strength of his own determination.

As he flipped the changer and dropped a record into place, Paige went to him. Her arms went around him from behind and she stroked the taut muscles of his stomach as her cheek rested against his back. "Would you mind very much if we made a few alterations in the evening's plans?"

The deep breath he drew beneath her hands echoed the tension inside her. "Pizza instead of egg rolls?" he asked with a trace of a sigh.

"Forget about food," she advised.

"Don't tell me you think you can exist on a night of conversation?"

"Forget about talking. Forget everything, except . . ." Music began, quietly surrounding them, shutting out the problems of the day and the world outside the door. He turned and she lifted her face to his, tempting his kiss. "Make love with me, Jeff."

His eyes darkened and his arms gathered her close. "Oh, Paige. . . ."

The pressure of her fingers at the back of his head brought him bending to capture her parted and willing lips. Pressing close and then even closer, she flattened herself against him, shaping, fitting, arching with the need to blend into one body, until there wasn't room for a single doubt between them.

Desire seared the hands that stroked her and whispered to her of the heat building inside him. It was inside her, too, the fire of loving and wanting and needing past the point of caution. She would be burned. Paige knew she couldn't avoid it. He felt so good, so beautifully, wondrously right in her arms.

He tugged at the waist of her slacks and slipped his hand inside the silk T-shirt she wore. Searching the pleasured satin of her skin, his fingers wandered upward to find the warm, waiting curve of her breast. She had wanted him countless times before, but now she ached with the desire to show him, to please him as his touch pleased her.

When he drew back and cupped her face in his hands, Paige stood breathlessly still, seeking the reflection of her own emotion in his eyes. It was there . . . and in the gentleness of his touch, as well as in the pensive line of his mouth. Jeff could deny the feeling for the rest of his life, but she knew he loved her.

Her fingers went weak as she placed them against his lips and felt him respond with the slightest pressure. Then he was bending, lifting her up and into his arms, holding her against his chest, and carrying her to the bedroom. There he laid her on the bed and plied her lips with moist, seeking kisses as he stretched out beside her.

It was a small bed, smaller with the two of them, and Paige took full advantage of the lack of space. She nestled against Jeff, letting her hands slide over his chest in sentient caress. Her chin tucked into the space below his chin and her hips found a promising haven. A quiet sound of need rumbled from his throat and she pressed her understanding to the pulse beating madly beneath her lips.

Sweet, trembling passion rose like an ocean wave and crested, rippling through her with intense and heady yearning. She kissed him without pattern, wanting only to taste and touch and tantalize. From shoulder to chin and along the determined line of his jaw she moved. At his ear she lingered to nip the lobe and to allow her tongue a teasing circle of intimacy. He shuddered and turned, burying his mouth in the hollows of her shoulder, discovering the pliant, silken skin awaiting his kiss.

She had no sensation of distance as they moved apart to strip away clothing. She had little sense of the soft give of the mattress as Jeff came to her again. All she knew, all she wanted to know, was him—the smooth texture of his back beneath her hand, the crisp feel of his chest against her breast, the seductive hardness of his thighs.

The music continued, but whether it was the records playing in the next room or simply the love song singing inside her head, Paige couldn't discern.

It was a familiar melody, winsome and sensuous and new because she was new. At last her heart was at peace. At last Jeff was again in her arms. And her world was finally coming aright.

He hadn't said. She hadn't asked. But she knew the unspoken commitment lay between them, sheltered and nurtured by the loving they now shared. The mending of their relationship wasn't complete, but in the shadowed darkness as Jeff touched her, caressed her, whispered quiet kisses that reached all the way to her heart, she knew it was healing.

With a sigh, she brought her hand to his cheek, her mouth to his and sealed the awareness that morning would awaken them together. New, as only true and lasting lovers could be, and willing to forget, forgive, and begin again. The music crescendoed, grew lyrically wistful, sensuously rhythmic, and then repeated the beautiful pattern until the world held nothing but Paige and Jeff and a love song.

CHAPTER EIGHT

Saturday dawned in a misty sunrise and by noon the day was cast in early summer gold. Paige wanted nothing so much as to enjoy the world from the vantage point of the backyard. With Jeff beside her, she thought she could have spent the entire weekend in delicious laziness.

Jeff seemed agreeable, but unfortunately Paige knew she couldn't avoid attending the afternoon buffet her mother had planned weeks before. Jeff, however, saw no reason he *shouldn't* avoid it. It took the whole morning to change his mind, and even then he only came to a reluctant agreement when she mentioned the abundance of culinary delights awaiting his tastebuds.

Paige kept her smile safely to herself, allowing him this minor deception. She didn't expect him to admit he would do something he really didn't want to do just to please her. But she knew, and the knowledge wrapped sweetly around her heart.

To give due credit to his epicurean appetites, Jeff wasn't shy about sampling the variety of food Mary had assembled for the party. But Paige noticed, too, how he stayed near her throughout most of the afternoon. It was only when she entered the kitchen at her mother's request for help that he moved on to join a quartet of old, and once close, friends.

"Jeff seems to be enjoying himself," Mary commented in the privacy of the white-tiled kitchen. "I'm glad he came with you, Paige."

"So am I." Paige opened the refrigerator door and peered inside. "What did you need out of here, anyway?"

"Nothing. I just wanted an excuse to have a mother-daughter talk. Since Jeff's return, I haven't seen much of you."

Letting the refrigerator close, Paige straightened to regard Mary's picture-perfect motherly smile. Her appearance was impeccable as usual, from the fashionable silk skirt and sweater she wore to the every-strand-in-place style of her blond hair. It was nice, Paige decided, to like the person who happened to be your mother. She and Mary certainly had experienced some rocky moments, but with maturity friendship had grown between them and Paige was especially grateful for the gift.

"What did you want to talk about?" she asked, although she knew what the answer would be.

"You."

What a typically maternal remark. "I'm fine. There's nothing to talk about."

"But he *is* here with you this afternoon."

"Largely due to the wonderful canapés and hors d'oeuvres you serve at these gatherings. You've noticed, I'm sure, the amount of time he's spent with a cracker in his hand."

"If we're going to talk about equal time, I think you're several minutes ahead of the buffet table."

Paige laughed low and soft in her throat. "Maybe so, but I'd hate to put his loyalty to the test."

"Putting the people you love to a test is always a mistake. It's a bit like eavesdropping—you're almost always bound to be disappointed."

It would have been easy to deny the need to talk, but suddenly Paige knew that was exactly what she wanted to do. How did mothers always know? Palms flat against the cool enamel door behind her, Paige prepared an answer for the question hidden in Mary's cautioning words. "Jeff has a lot of hurt left, Mom. I realize more every time I'm with him how much I contributed to that. A few months ago I would never have admitted, or even believed, that I'd tested his love for me over and over during our marriage, but now . . ." She crossed her ankles and studied the leather toe strap of one sandal. "I never appreciated all the compromises he made for me. I was so sure I was making his life better, happier." Shaking her head, she met Mary's concerned eyes. "I just didn't understand . . . so very many things."

Mary smiled a loving reassurance. "Marriage is hard work and you were young, Paige. Not so much in years as in experience. You grew up believing that life was a helium balloon filled with dreams come true and you held the string."

"But that's no excuse, Mother. When Jeff needed my support and encouragement, I failed him. I didn't understand. I didn't even try. All he wanted was for me to believe in him, to trust him, but I . . ."

Mary moved to touch Paige's shoulder. "Don't be so hard on yourself. Of course, you made mistakes. So did Jeff. Both of you are strong-willed and temperamental. Clash was inevitable."

"Sometimes I think the divorce was too."

"If you believed that, you wouldn't be here talking about it and Jefferson Lawrence wouldn't be outside waiting for you right now."

That was inarguable, yet the uncertainty, the restlessness, that shadowed her every mood made her cautious. "But it might not mean anything, Mother."

"It means something. Maybe not what you want it to mean, but . . ." Mary gave Paige a quick hug. "I wish I could give you a guarantee, dear, but there just aren't any. You cut the cards, took the risk, and brought him back—even if it is only temporarily. Maybe you ought to consider the chances he took in coming back."

In a swift return to normal, lighthearted concern, Mary gently pushed Paige from in front of the refrigerator. "Let's have something to drink before we go back to being hostess's daughter. With any luck at all . . ." She looked inside the refrigerator and smiled her pleasure. "Ah, a wine spritzer. Just what you need to keep that man away from my buffet table."

Paige didn't know how a glass of wine for her would have any noticeable effect on Jeff's appetite, but if her mother thought so, then she was certainly willing to give it a try.

It took slightly less than five minutes with his four old buddies—one heavyset, one tall, one with glasses, and one without—for Jeff to remember why he'd never really belonged with this particular group of friends. Once he and Paige had been a part of the set made up of these men and their wives, talking in endless, meaningless circles about too many bills, too little salary, and not enough time. On reflection, though, Jeff realized he'd never had much in common with any of them. He didn't understand the dissatisfaction that bound the group together, but he knew a sense of relief that he had outgrown it and them. His dissatisfaction was of a more personal nature and would, one way or another, be resolved soon. In response to the thought, his gaze turned toward the kitchen doorway. Paige was still inside, out of sight but not out of mind, and he felt an indefinite pleasure in the knowledge.

"I'll bet Glendenning wasn't any too happy to see you," one of the quartet said, bringing Jeff's thoughts reluctantly back to the group.

"Gary? Oh, I doubt it made a great deal of difference to him. We hardly knew each other, anyway."

There was a hearty chuckle from the heavyset man on Jeff's right. "You can't kid us, Lawrence. We remember the time you put that cowboy down for the count. Not that he didn't deserve it, but—"

"That happened a long time ago. I'm sure he's forgotten all about it." Jeff paused and added pointedly, "And I'd certainly like to."

This time the chuckles circled all the men. Jeff was the only one who saw no humor in the conversation. "Even if he doesn't remember the way you licked him in that wrestling match," the tallest of the four said, "he hasn't forgotten that you got his girl. When his dad married Mary Randall and acquired the executive suite and Paige as a stepdaughter, Gary must have thought he had things sewed up. I heard Edward really pushed a match between Paige and his son—until you came along."

"That's right." It was Dave, the one with glasses. "I'll bet old man Glendenning hated you as much as Gary did. He could have had a real family business going—his son, his stepdaughter—all one big, happy electronics firm. After the divorce, hopes must have run pretty high again, but now that you're back, well . . ."

Jeff couldn't believe the stupidity running rampant among a group of so-called professional men, but he thought it best to resist stating his opinion. "You guys have made one too many trips to the bar this afternoon," he said lightly, and started to walk away.

"Just the same," one of them—he neither knew nor cared who—called after him, "if I were you, I'd keep my backside covered."

Quite a conversation, Jeff thought, and wondered how Paige would have reacted. She would have laughed, he decided after a few minutes of consideration. Jeff felt rather proud that his response had been calm this time. It would have been easy to lose his temper. He hadn't appreciated the comments that had been made and he had resented the slur against Edward. Over the years he'd had plenty of reasons to disagree with his former father-in-law, but never a doubt that Edward wanted Paige to be happy. Of course, there was some truth to the idea that Edward had hoped Paige would choose his son over any other suitors and that he'd been disappointed when she had chosen Jeff instead.

Was there also some truth behind the idea that Edward had hoped she would turn to Gary after the divorce? Jeff didn't have time to consider that before Paige came into view and he lost track of time and place. How could just the sight of her affect him so, especially after all that had happened? But it did, and he was no longer fool enough to deny it. He walked toward her, his smile beginning deep inside his heart.

"Would you mind leaving a little early?" he asked when he reached her.

"How early?" Her smile went soft with welcome, silky with unspoken suggestion. "And why?"

"Now, because I've had all the reminiscing with the old gang that I can handle for a while."

"Didn't you enjoy seeing them again?"

"Seeing them wasn't so bad. *Listening* to them was what got to me."

Paige patted his arm. "They haven't grown up yet, have they?"

He was surprised by her perception. At one time, Paige had fiercely defended their friends against what she had called his unreasonable attitudes. "It's probably more likely that you and I have changed and, good or bad, we've outgrown them."

"It's good, Jeff. Maybe if we'd spent a little less time with them and more with each other . . ." It was a futile wish, as most wishes were, but he took her hand and Paige was glad she'd voiced the thoughts aloud. "What did they say?" she asked.

"A few off-the-wall remarks about Gary and you. Nothing worth repeating."

"Any remark linking me with Gary would have to be off-the-wall."

Jeff lifted a skeptical brow. "But you have been dating him."

"Not dating, really. Gary's good company . . . sometimes. I've known him a long time, and although I don't regard him as a brother, he is family. Sort of."

"Very convincing, Paige," Jeff said sarcastically, but he smiled a contradictory amusement. "You didn't see him much when you were growing up, did you?"

"No. Gary resented Edward's marriage to Mother and he had no interest in building a relationship with his stepfamily. When I was old enough to be interesting, he had a sudden change of heart." She laughed quietly. "At least toward me. He still wouldn't have much to do with Edward. I suppose that's one reason I never told Gary to get lost. Edward wanted to be close to his son and I always felt I was his one link of communication."

"Are you still?"

"In a way I guess I am. Does that bother you?" She turned questioning eyes to his face.

"No." He offered reassurance by squeezing her hand, but something *was* bothering him, some nameless, nagging riddle that he couldn't quite pin down. "Is the relationship between Edward and Gary getting any better?"

A noncommittal answer tucked in the corner of her mouth. "I don't really see much improvement. They can talk to each other now for brief, unemotional periods, but Gary doesn't let anyone get very close and that goes double for Edward."

Paige stopped, her gaze circling the room, looking for her stepfather, checking the possibility that he might be close enough to overhear. When she saw him across the room, she leaned closer to Jeff and whispered, "That's why I can't believe Gary was involved in the theft of those papers, Jeff. I just can't see him allowing Sandi or anyone else to help him, much less support him—no matter what style he's grown accustomed to living in."

Jeff made no comment, although he reluctantly conceded her point. Still, he couldn't quite absolve Gary Glendenning from suspicion. Too many parts of the puzzle were coming together and the developing picture implicated Gary, but there was no point in making Paige face that until it became a probability.

The feeling of protectiveness was familiar and oddly comforting. Jeff glanced at Paige, noted the soft glow of happiness in her eyes, on her cheeks, and he knew he wanted always to see her that way. The risk of being hurt again seemed less and less important next to the risk of living without her. He had done that already. He could do it again, if necessary. But in that quiet moment, amid a room full of inconsequential chatter, Jeff admitted he didn't want to.

"You didn't answer my question," he said, leaning down to inhale the sensuous fragrance of her perfume.

Her eyes widened at the seductive tone of his gesture. "What question?"

"The one about leaving early."

"Oh. Do you have plans for the evening?"

"Yes, and so do you." His breath caressed her shoulder with his intention, and her heart fluttered in her throat.

"In that case, I think we ought to leave as soon as possible."

"You always were a sensible woman, Paige."

Her lips curved in pleasurable argument. "Not always, but I'm learning."

Hand in hand, they strolled away from the room, the party, and anyone with the bad manners to try to delay them. In the car Jeff managed to keep possession of her hand and her heart. Nothing was said until he drove into the driveway of her house and parked.

He turned to her then and ran a tentative finger along her palm. "Why did you insist on offering the Tri-Star consultation to me, Paige?"

She bent her head. "I told you—"

"No, that isn't what I meant. I want to know the real reason, the personal reason."

Silence lingered between them, presenting itself as neither friend nor foe, but simply as a gathering place for courage. "I wanted you back, Jeff."

"Why?"

She had rehearsed this moment a hundred times, what she would tell him, how she would feel. Now the words she'd practiced vanished. She didn't know how to say what had to be said. Releasing her breath, she inhaled again and lifted her chin, meeting his eyes with all the honesty and composure she possessed. "Because once I stopped being angry and lonely, I realized I wasn't going to stop loving you or get past the point of being unhappy without you."

He was supposed to say something like *I love you,*

or *I've been unhappy without you, too.* She had imagined it so many times—not just her part, but his response as well. And now the only sound she heard was the fierce pounding of her heart. He still held her hand, but she didn't know if he even realized it.

"Paige. . . ." His thumb made a slow circle against her wrist. "I accepted the job with Randall Electronics for one reason—to find out what had happened to the NaeComp papers. The day I received the letter from Edward, I wasn't unhappy with my life and I—" He cleared his throat, but the huskiness remained. "—I thought I had stopped loving you. I wanted it that way."

And now . . .

The question hung in the silence, just as she poised on the edge of a fragile hope. *Oh, Jeff,* she thought, *please give us a chance. Please let me love you again.* But she couldn't ask. It had to be his choice.

"I don't want it to be that way anymore, Paige. There are a lot of things we need to talk about, some feelings we need to resolve. But before we can do that, I have to finish what I came here to do. I have to prove once and for all that I had nothing to do with the theft."

"Not for me, Jeff. I always believed you were innocent. It was only the circumstances, the timing—"

"I have to do this for me, Paige."

It was the first time she truly appreciated the new maturity he had earned in the past two years. He was calm, confident, determined, and she loved him more than she'd ever thought possible.

"I understand, Jeff." She curled her fingers around his as her lips found a slow, sure happiness. "Let's go inside," she suggested softly. "I have plans for you."

The somber expression in his dark eyes faded to a sweet, gentle amusement. "I was hoping you would."

"It comes from being a sensible woman, you know."

"I didn't know, but I have a feeling you're going to tell me."

"No." Paige reached across him and opened his car door. "I'm going to *show* you. . . ."

He didn't waste any time in giving her all the opportunity she needed.

CHAPTER NINE

Saturday's golden charm turned into a windy midnight and became a full-fledged midwestern squall early Sunday morning. Thunder cracked at frequent intervals, lightning ripped through the darkness, and the wind howled like a banshee's cry. Jeff lay awake, wondering how Paige could sleep, remembering all the times during their marriage when she'd roused him and asked the same thing.

Storms didn't bother him. Given the choice, he preferred the temperamental Oklahoma weather to the steady, year-round warmth of vacation climates. Tonight, though, he was bothered by the emotional storm brewing around him. It was just a feeling, a heavy sort of apprehension, but Jeff knew intuitively that something was about to happen.

He glanced at Paige dreaming peacefully beside him. She had changed. Certainly, he was a very different person than he'd been when he'd first loved her. But would those changes be enough? Oddly, he felt more of a commitment to her now than he'd ever felt before, but he knew the sacrifices involved in trying to build a new relationship. Paige would have to make some concessions and the last time he'd asked her to do that . . .

On cue, his memory provided the scene. He'd told her he was ready to make a change. He'd told her about his plans for opening the consulting firm. He'd told her it would mean moving to Oklahoma City. She'd told him no, no, and no. It had ended with an argument, an ultimatum, and the slamming of the front door behind him.

Now it seemed a childish way to make such an important decision, but at the time, Jeff had felt compelled to sever the ties that made him dependent on Paige. His resignation from Randall Electronics wasn't impulsive; he'd contemplated the idea for months. He understood now, though, how his actions had appeared hasty and unplanned—even to Paige, who had known what he wanted to do. But she had been very good then at seeing only what she chose to see, at pretending all was well simply because she wanted it to be.

Why hadn't he seen that she was afraid, that his dissatisfaction with every area of his life threatened her security? He had been in an emotional turmoil, wanting to break away from job, friends, hometown, and family ties—all the things she valued so much. He'd asked—no, he'd *told*—her she would have to leave all those things behind.

Given the same circumstances today, Jeff knew he would handle the situation—and Paige—differently.

He'd gained self-confidence in the past two years. He'd learned that his career wasn't dependent on the financial and professional security that being married to Paige had brought into his life. He had survived, and that in itself had been worth the cost. If only the price hadn't been Paige and the simple faith he'd always believed she had for him.

She stirred as the thunder rumbled again, and Jeff shifted onto his side to look at her. A wave of tenderness rocked him as he brushed a strand of dark hair from her forehead. The opportunity to love again was within reach and he felt a little awed by the prospect. Second chances so rarely happened, and he would not let happiness elude him again. No matter what kind of storm threatened, come the morning, Paige would be beside him.

"It must have rained last night." Paige looked out the window at a lawn glistening wet beneath the rising sun.

"It did," Jeff said, without looking up from the morning paper. "You slept right through the show—thunder, lightning, wind, rain. You missed the whole thing."

"Why didn't you wake me?"

"I didn't want to have to get out of bed to listen to weather reports."

She turned from the window to regard the bare feet propped on one end of her sofa. She supposed his back was propped against the other end, but the newspaper in his hands blocked the confirming view. All she could see were his fingers, curled around the edges of the paper, his feet, and the length of denim-clad legs in between. "You have no imagination, Jefferson Lawrence."

"But I do have an excellent memory, Eleanor Paige."

"You know I hate that name," she complained to the lingerie ad on the back of the newspaper.

"I can call you 'darlin',' if you prefer."

Frowning, she moved to stand beside the couch. "Maybe I'd prefer you to call me long distance."

One edge of the paper came down. "For someone who had a good night's sleep, you're a bit testy, aren't you?"

Placing one knee on the edge of the sofa, she slowly straddled his thighs and pulled the paper from his grasp to drop it onto the floor. "As I said, you have no imagination."

The surprise in his eyes was quickly replaced by a warm, dark welcome, and his hands went to her shoulders in soft caress. "Smile when you say that."

She didn't. Seduction was a serious matter, and Paige proceeded to convince him of her sincerity. She lowered her head, tempting his lips with the tip of her tongue. Slowly, making as much contact as possible, she contoured her body to match his position. She wanted him and every movement she made communicated that desire. Pleasing him, touching him, was her only thought, yet the feel of him beneath her, the fierce pounding of her heart, pleased her far more than she could ever hope to pleasure him.

Jeff was a fast learner and, with one hand at her hips and the other wrapped in the dusky silk of her hair, he opened his mouth to her seeking kiss. Paige sighed with the warmth of his breath, surrendering to him a part of the responsibility for this most lovely seduction. Her senses filled to capacity with the touch and the scent and the taste of him, then overflowed to pool deep inside her.

When the telephone rang, Jeff left her lips to nuzzle a kiss behind her ear. "Ignore it," he whispered. "It'll go away."

She took his advice to heart and eventually the irritating sound stopped. It came again, inconveniently several minutes later, and then again a few minutes after that. Finally, during the next interlude of silence, Jeff released Paige just long enough to reach behind him and knock the receiver off the hook. "Now," he said as he feathered new kisses across her cheek, "what did you say about no imagination?"

"I was wrong," she murmured against his lips. "You're wonderfully creati—"

He persuaded her to communicate the rest of her opinion in more tangible ways. . . .

The telephone receiver didn't find its way back into place until much later in the day. Jeff dropped it onto the cradle as he walked past on his way to the kitchen. It rang before he'd taken three steps in that direction and he backtracked to answer it.

"Jeff?" The voice was male, vaguely familiar, and audibly relieved when Jeff confirmed his identity. "This is Ken Brown. Toby gave me this number, but I've been trying to reach you all morning and was beginning to think it wasn't right."

A puzzled frown tightened Jeff's lips. "Is there a problem, Ken? I finished the report on your computer malfunction and you should receive it sometime this next week. Toby said you didn't need it until—"

"I have it, Jeff. That's why I'm calling."

The frown deepened. "You mean you hired some other consultant to do it for you?"

"No, Jeff." Ken's voice sounded strained despite the distance. "I have the report *you* wrote. It was delivered to my office yesterday."

"Saturday?" Jeff clarified the day because it somehow seemed important. He wasn't sure why. "That's speedy delivery, Ken, considering the envelope was on my desk when I left work Friday evening."

"It came one-day express to Oklahoma City and I happened to be in the office when it arrived."

"But that's . . ." Jeff didn't even know where to start questioning what Ken was telling him.

"There's more, Jeff. When I opened the envelope I found some spec sheets that . . . uh, had no business being in the same room, much less the same envelope, as the report you did for me."

A sick feeling churned in his stomach and Jeff held the receiver with a death grip. "Tri-Star?" he asked hoarsely, and waited, knowing already what the answer would be, would *have* to be.

"Yes."

The churning became a vast, empty pocket of questions. "No identifying marks? Anything that might—?"

"Nothing. Only your handwriting on the front of the envelope."

God, he'd forgotten about that, but what did it matter anyway? His handwriting on that envelope was the least of the moment's problems. "Did you say anything to Toby?"

"I haven't told anyone, Jeff. I know what kind of trouble this spells, not only for you, but for me. My name and my company's name is on that envelope along with yours. If you fall under suspicion, so will I."

"I don't think so, Ken. This one is meant for me." Jeff pressed unsteady fingers to his forehead, trying to think, trying desperately to understand what he didn't want to understand. "I'll be there in a couple of hours to get the specs. Are you at your office? Never mind, give me a number to call when I get into town."

Ken gave the telephone number without hesitation. "I won't let these out of my sight—or into anyone else's—until then."

"Thank you, Ken. If you hadn't called—"

"Just get here and take the grenade out of my hand, would you? And, Jeff, I hope you've got your backside covered on this."

"So do I." Jeff offered another thank you before his fingers lost their grip on the receiver and it fell with a clatter onto the telephone base. He stared sightlessly at the floor, going over the information, knowing it would make sense to him eventually.

"Jeff?" Paige stood in the doorway and he met her concern reluctantly.

The old fear drifted through him and he felt hollow, caught between past and present. He was afraid to tell her and risk seeing suspicion cloud the new beginning they'd made. But she had to know and so did he. "That was a friend of mine, Ken Brown. He's an engineer in Oklahoma City and I just did a report on a computer malfunction for his firm." Jeff swallowed the tightness in his throat. "When I left the office Friday, it was on my desk ready to be mailed. Yesterday it was delivered to Ken."

An uncertain shiver trickled down her spine and Paige braced a shoulder against the door facing.

"Paige, the Tri-Star spec sheets were in the envelope."

Somehow, she had known he was going to say something like that, and yet surprise accelerated her heartbeat. "And you're supposed to take the blame," she said in breathy protest, "just like before."

"Not quite. This time the evidence would be more than circumstantial."

She nodded a solemn acknowledgment, although she couldn't absorb the magnitude of what was happening. That someone was not only stealing information from Randall Electronics but deliberately implicating Jeff was a truth she found hard to accept. Yet she knew it had to be faced. "The light you saw in the office window Friday when you left work—do you think—?"

"What else could it be? *I* didn't mail that envelope, so someone else had to have picked it up after I left."

"Mitch or Sandi. You saw both of them leave."

Jeff pushed restless fingers through his hair and then impatiently thrust the hand into his trouser pocket. "I think we can eliminate Mitch now. If he'd been selling information for the past couple of years, he'd be crazy to mess up a lucrative second income just because he doesn't like me. This theft was never meant to go undetected, Paige."

She sighed and walked to his side. Her hand sought to give and receive comfort in the warmth of his palm. "No, you're right. Someone"—she paused and forced herself to name the thief—"Sandi intended the papers to turn up missing on Monday morning, and since you're in charge of the Tri-Star Project . . ."

"I'd be the first one questioned. And somehow, someone would know about the envelope being mailed, special delivery, to Ken."

The room went silent with suppositions, but Paige and Jeff both knew the scenario would have been the same as two years before. "How could Sandi have known that Ken wouldn't take advantage of the situation and sell the information?"

"It wouldn't make any difference, Paige. Sandi's objective was to create a security leak within Randall Electronics. The only way she can help Gary is to funnel contracts to his company. She's probably been leaking bids like the one for the Clemons contract to him for the past twenty-four months, if not longer. Hasn't he been wooing some of your clients away from you?"

"Well, yes, a few, but Gary wouldn't—"

"Stop protecting him, Paige. If he isn't in on this—and I don't see how he couldn't be—we'll find out soon enough."

"Are you driving to Oklahoma City to get the papers?"

"Yes. Come tomorrow morning, I'm going to be ready."

"I want to go with you."

He squeezed her hand. "It's a two-hour drive. Did you think for one minute I'd leave you behind?"

She stepped into his arms and held him tightly. It was frightening to think of Sandi as being so calculating. Paige lifted her chin and met Jeff's dark eyes. "Why, Jeff? Why would she do it? Why would Gary . . . ?"

"I wish I had the answer."

"I wish I knew how she got around all the safeguards we use. How could she just walk out with those papers? Gary couldn't go anywhere near the security vault."

Jeff's arm tightened around her waist. "We'll find out in the morning, Paige. I'm not sure how, but tomorrow we're going to do what we should have done two years ago. We're going to get to the bottom of these thefts—the when, what, where, why, and how."

"I guess we ought to phone Edward and let him know what's happened."

"I think we better pick up those spec sheets first. Until they're back where they're supposed to be, the situation is potentially explosive and I'm not going to get caught in it a second time."

"You won't, Jeff. We won't let that happen again."

It was a promise in her azure eyes, a gentle assurance in her voice, and relief flowed through him. He cupped her chin in his hands and touched her lips with his own. There was so much he wanted to tell her, so many different emotions he would have liked to communicate, but it would have to wait. "Let's go, Paige. I want to put all of this behind us."

"I'm ready." She took another kiss from the corner of his mouth before pulling back with a sigh. "Are you going to invite me to see your etchings while we're in the city?"

He smiled in wry amusement. "Don't underestimate my imagination. I have a much better line than that."

"Let's hear it."

"Later. For now, we have things to do and—"

"—places to go. I know." She turned and walked to the doorway. "I'll put on some shoes and meet you at the car."

"Paige?"

She glanced over her shoulder.

"I love you."

A sweet rush of emotion closed her throat and misted in her eyes. Her lips trembled with a smile. "I think this could be the longest trip I've ever taken to Oklahoma City."

His answering smile was tenderly understanding and Paige hugged it to her heart. It lingered there in a warming glow during the drive from Tulsa to Oklahoma City. At first, the silence they shared was filled with thoughts of a distant future, but as the miles slipped past, Paige found her mind going over the reasons for their trip. Everywhere she turned, a new question confronted her and when she finally put the thoughts into words, Jeff's quick comprehension told her he'd been thinking along the same lines.

"I don't understand why Sandi would take such a risk, Jeff. She worked hard to obtain her engineering degree and you know how proud she is of her own work. She just isn't the type to count the world well lost for love."

"There isn't going to be a pat explanation, Paige. Motivations for this kind of corporate theft are as many and varied as the people who perpetrate it. Maybe Gary has promised her the sky in return for the information. Maybe she's simply jealous of you and this is her way of punishing you for having the advantages she never had. We may never know."

"I guess you're right." Paige frowned as she turned her gaze to the scenery along the highway. "But I can't help wondering how she ever got past Gary's independence. He's so *careful* about giving any appearance of accepting help . . . in any form. Edward tried so many times and was refused outright, no matter how much Gary might have needed the assistance. I can't understand . . ." She let the words trail away, knowing Jeff was right. She probably would never be able to understand.

As the pensive quiet settled around him, Jeff experienced an unsettling tension in his stomach. The nagging uncertainties, the endless string of questions, spun through his mind and slowly formed a pattern he did not want to recognize. But there it was. Like the colored bits of glass in a kaleidoscope, all the pieces fell into perfect order and he didn't know how he could have missed seeing the answer for so long.

CHAPTER TEN

The air in Edward's office was stuffy and Jeff couldn't rid himself of the heavy feeling in his lungs. Paige didn't seem to be bothered, but then she didn't know what was coming. Jeff frowned. He wasn't sure he knew, either.

All night the same questions had chased themselves through his mind, around and around, and always the answer came out the same: Edward Glendenning. Jeff didn't want it to be true, but it all fit together too neatly to be denied. Edward had the motivation—a father's concern for his son's well-being. Edward had the opportunity—he knew Randall Electronics inside and out. He had access to all information within the company. He was, with the exception of Paige, the last person anyone would suspect.

And Jeff didn't know how in hell he was going to prove his suspicion had any basis in fact. Edward had the ability and the means to cover his tracks and there was little doubt that he'd done exactly that. Without concrete evidence, Jeff knew it would be simply his word against Edward's. Not quite the exoneration of guilt he'd hoped to accomplish when he'd decided to come back to Randall Electronics. Not quite the proof of innocence he'd wanted to present to Paige.

He looked at her, sitting so still and composed in the chair next to him. She was a bit pale and there was an aura of fragility about her on this Monday morning. Strain, of course, and worry about Edward's reaction to the news they were waiting to tell him. Jeff told himself he was a fool for not preparing her, but from the moment he'd realized Edward, not Sandi and Gary, was responsible for the thefts, he hadn't been able to find the words.

Paige had been quietly accepting of the unpleasant task ahead of them. Yesterday they'd gone straight to Ken's home and picked up the stolen TriStar spec sheets. She'd been a little pale then too. Jeff had noticed the careful way she handled the envelope and the betraying tension around her mouth. Without a word, she'd conveyed to him the mixture of emotions she felt. He knew that until that moment, until she actually held the proof in her hands, she'd hoped it would all turn out to be a mistake. He'd watched her then and he'd understood the anger and disillusionment she faced. And he hadn't had the courage to add to her disappointment by suggesting Edward might be involved.

He watched her now and still he couldn't bring himself to tell her.

"How long have we been waiting?" she asked and he turned a facsimile of a smile in her direction.

"About ten minutes longer than when you last asked. He'll be here soon, I'm sure." Jeff didn't know what would happen when Edward did arrive at his office. He hoped something in the conversation, some hidden inspiration, would spark the truth. "It's barely past eight-thirty now."

Her lips tipped ruefully. "But it's been a long night."

He thought it had been far too fleeting. After getting the papers, he'd taken her to his office and then to his home in Oklahoma City. After dinner, he'd suggested driving back to Tulsa and she'd agreed. Although she didn't mention it, Jeff had known she understood his reasons, his reluctance to chance any repetition of the scene two years before when he'd been delayed and had walked straight into a steambath of accusation.

She'd fallen asleep on the way home and Jeff had struggled with his conscience. How could he confide his suspicion, his gut feeling, that Edward was guilty of theft and corporate sabotage? How could he put Paige in the position of having to choose loyalties? It was the same kind of emotional conflict as before, and in the end Jeff had decided he couldn't tell her of Edward's guilt, any more than he'd been able to tell her of his own innocence then. If she didn't see it for herself, any words he said would be only hollow truths.

Selfishly, he'd clung to that decision, wanting to have the night unmarred by the disillusionment that morning would bring. It had been easy to interpret an unspoken request in Paige's expression and voice as a plea for forgetfulness, a beseeching look as a need for solace.

He had held her through the night and she had held him. There had been no mention of the future, no reference to the unpleasant morning awaiting them, but Jeff wouldn't have traded those moments of sharing for anything in the world.

Restlessly, he rose and paced to the paneled wall where awards and plaques hung in places of honor. Honor—Jeff wasn't sure he knew what it meant anymore. In this very room he had once refused to defend his integrity, and honor had been sacrificed to stubborn pride. Now, in this same room, he had to challenge Edward, a man Jeff respected and admired, the stepfather Paige loved. For a moment, Jeff fought the tight knot of protest in his throat and then he let the disappointment flow freely. It was a no-win situation—for Edward, for Paige, and for himself. Everyone was going to lose. Jeff pushed his palm flat against the wall and reluctantly accepted the price honor now demanded of him.

Paige watched in concern, aware of Jeff's tension, knowing the cause, yet sensing an intangible threat in his silence. With a sigh, she ran a finger along the edge of the brown envelope in her lap. Inside, the Tri-Star spec sheets lay waiting to give mute testimony to the crime committed against Randall Electronics and against Jeff by Sandi Winners and possibly Gary Glendenning as well. Paige didn't relish the telling of any part of the story, but most of all, she dreaded telling Edward about Gary.

Jeff was right, though, she knew. It was time to take action, to stop the thefts and the leakage of information for whatever reason, no matter who was involved or how unpleasant the situation became. That, after all, was the reason for being in Edward's office. She wished her stepfather hadn't chosen this particular Monday to be late. It seemed as if she and Jeff had been here for hours.

She brought her gaze to him again; noted the stiffness in his shoulders and the way he braced his hand against the wall. There was something she didn't understand, but she didn't know where to begin searching for what it might be. Suddenly the closeness in the room, the dread, the restlessness of the past several hours caught her and her head spun with a dizzy feeling of déjà vu.

But no, this was not the same as before, she told herself. This time she was not separated from Jeff by misguided intentions and misunderstandings. He loved her. She loved him. Nothing would change that. She simply wouldn't allow it.

"Paige?" Edward entered the room with a question. He approached her and dropped a kiss to her cheek. "I'm glad you received my message this morning."

Her brows lifted, but she couldn't quite manage a smile. "I didn't, Edward. When did you—?"

"I phoned you at home, but there wasn't an answer. So I left word with your secretary that I needed to see you as soon as possible." He looked worried in a distracted sort of way, but as he caught sight of Jeff the expression changed. "Jeff," he said without enthusiasm, "I didn't leave a message for you, but since you're here . . ."

"I'll stay, thanks."

Paige felt the animosity vibrating through the room like the echo of a hand slapping a face. She looked from Jeff to Edward and back again, confused by the tension between these two men. Edward recovered his composure first. "That might be a good idea."

As he walked behind the desk and seated himself in the oversized leather chair, Paige swallowed her apprehensions and leaned forward. "Edward, Jeff and I wanted to talk to you about—we thought you ought to know—" She couldn't finish and for the first time in years she felt the awkward gap of communication that had existed in the early stages of her relationship with her stepfather. How should she begin? She glanced at Jeff and he responded by moving to stand behind her chair. His hands cupped her shoulders and she felt calmer.

Edward's gaze flicked from Jeff's reassuring gesture to her face. "You two are getting back together," he stated flatly. "If that's what you want, Paige, then

I'm happy for you. But there is something I think we ought to clear up." He paused and absently tapped an indecisive finger on the desk top. The lines around his eyes deepened to thoughtful crevices and his mouth wrinkled with a frown before he fixed a steady regard on Paige. "I'm sorry to have to tell you this, dear, but there's been another . . . incident."

"No, Edward, the—" The pressure on her shoulders cut off her explanation and she looked up at Jeff. His whole attention, though, was centered on the older man.

"Incident?" Jeff's voice was coolly interested, but the fingers pressing into her upper arms were anything but casual. Paige slowly turned back around as she tried to grasp the reason for the silent warning.

Edward met the challenge without hesitation. "Another theft, Jefferson. It seems that when security ran the morning file check, some specification sheets are missing."

"Let me guess," Jeff said, his tone still confusingly unconcerned. "The Tri-Star project has sprung a leak."

"I didn't mention any file name." Edward lifted a corner of his mouth in an austere smile. "You shouldn't jump to conclusions." He shifted his focus to Paige. "There is cause for concern, though. We can't let word of this latest mistake"—the glance he flicked to Jeff's face sent a chill of familiar anxiety through Paige and her fingers creased the envelope she held—"get around until we have more information."

"A minute ago you said there had been another theft, Edward." Jeff spoke before Paige had a chance to ask a question. "Now you're calling it a mistake. I don't want to jump to conclusions here, so why don't you clarify the problem for us? Has something been stolen? Or just misplaced?"

She didn't understand what was happening, but a formless doubt kept her silent, listening, waiting for someone to mention Sandi's involvement.

"If classified information is not in the vault, Jeff, then it could hardly be misplaced, could it?"

"You're sure it isn't in the vault?"

Edward clasped thin hands together, palm to palm, fingertip to fingertip. "I wouldn't have mentioned it to Paige if I'd thought otherwise."

Jeff was unfazed by the caustic note in her stepfather's voice. "And I'm sure you have no idea where those spec sheets might be."

Animosity crackled around her and Paige hardly dared to breathe. Edward straightened his posture and his dignity. "There's no need to be so defensive, Jeff. No one has accused you of anything."

"No one *accused* me of stealing the NaeComp information either, but that didn't stop you from letting me take the blame for it." The pressure on her shoulders increased and Paige covered one of Jeff's hands with her hand. Immediately, the pressure eased. "I won't do that again, Edward."

"You made your own choices, son."

"But my choice certainly suited your purpose, didn't it, Edward?"

"Jeff!" Paige pulled forward in the chair and turned sideways so that she could see both men. She didn't know the reason for this tug-of-war, but she thought it ought to stop now. "Let's concentrate on the problem we have this morning, all right? Edward, Jeff and I have been waiting for you because we already knew about the Tri-Star spec sheets. We have th—"

"But how could you know?" Edward pushed back his chair and rose, his hands supporting him as he leaned across the desk toward her. "Security only notified me a little while ago and I—" He looked hard at Jeff. "Unless, of course . . . ?"

Insinuation was implicit in the suggestive way the sentence trailed into silence. Paige was shocked by her stepfather's behavior. She had never seen him lose control, but he seemed very close to doing just that. An elusive question slipped through her mind, but she couldn't bring it into focus. Jeff took a step forward and Paige stood, placing herself between the angry glares being exchanged by the men. "Jeff," she whispered hoarsely, "what are you doing?"

Jeff inhaled deeply and relaxed his fists. "Paige has the spec sheets, Edward."

The announcement hung suspended on the edge of silence for a fraction of a second. "How did you get them?"

Paige glanced at Jeff, but when he made no attempt to answer, she took the initiative. "They were mailed in the same envelope with a report Jeff had done. The recipient of the envelope called as soon as he discovered the spec sheets."

"So you drove to Oklahoma City yesterday and recovered them." Edward spoke quietly and Paige felt a moment's concern for his unnatural pallor.

"Yes," she said, "Jeff and I decided—" The words froze in her throat as her mind grappled with sudden comprehension. Her gaze dropped to the envelope she still held in her hands . . . the address was concealed from view and she hadn't turned it over since first entering the office. She raised a troubled look to her stepfather. "How did you know the papers were in Oklahoma City?"

Jeff's hand gripped her shoulder again, but she was hardly aware of his touch. All she could see was Edward and the endless, awful possibilities spinning inside her head. An eternity might have come and gone as she held his gaze and hoped against hope he would have an explanation. When the seconds lengthened to a condemning minute and then another, her hope—and a bit of her innocence—died. Edward seemed to realize it, too. He swallowed and she watched him sink slowly to the edge of his chair.

"I mailed the envelope." The admission was weak, unlike Edward's usually confident tones, and yet how like him it was not to make any attempt at denial. "I—never meant for this to happen, Paige."

She was cold. So very cold. "How could you, Edward? How could you steal from Mother and from me? Why?"

"Gary needed help, Paige. His company was floundering and I knew it. He didn't tell me. He never told me anything, never asked for help, but I heard about the trouble and I—" The look in his faded blue eyes insisted on her understanding. "I had to help him, Paige. There was nothing else I could do."

"I can't believe Gary wanted you to steal in order to—"

"Gary doesn't know. I've been very careful, Paige. I set up the security leak two years ago because I knew Gary's company had been second low bidder on the NaeComp contract. It was a simple matter to destroy the spec sheets and let everyone believe they'd been stolen. NaeComp withdrew that contract and took their business to Gary. We didn't really need it anyway. Randall Electronics has always had more business than we can handle."

She felt sick. This wasn't the loving stepfather she'd always known. This couldn't be the moral man she knew so well sitting there talking about an immoral situation as if it were perfectly innocent. How had he been able to rationalize his guilt into a sequence of logic that was perfectly justified in his own mind? "Edward, we almost got sued over that contract. How could you believe—" She made herself stop. What would arguing accomplish? "Gary must know, Edward. How else did you get the information about his company's bid?"

"I have a contact there." Edward clenched his hands on the desk top. "Gary doesn't have any idea that I've been helping him and I want to keep it that way."

She sank to the edge of her chair, unable to accept the illogic in his thinking. Didn't he realize the consequences of his actions? Didn't he know Gary would *have* to know? And her mother? Oh, God, her mother. Paige began to tremble and Jeff stepped forward, shielding her from the necessity of asking the questions that still had to be asked. "How long have you been helping Gary like this? Are the NaeComp specs the only papers you destroyed?"

Edward pursed his lips in a sullen gesture at odds with his sad attempt to maintain his dignity. "NaeComp was the first. I didn't have to go to that extreme again. It was easier after that just to overbid a few contracts. Of course, it didn't always work out. Sometimes a competitor underbid both Randall Electronics and Gary's company. But overall it worked out well." Edward caught Paige's gaze again in a look that blended apology and explanation. "No one got hurt. This company is still in great shape. Gary's company is holding its own and the contracting companies haven't suffered any injury."

Paige stiffened with righteous anger. "What about the injury you caused Jeff? And me? What about our marriage, Edward? How can you say no one was hurt?"

"I didn't intend to hurt you, Paige. You know I'd never do that deliberately. Jeff got in the way last time with his sudden decision to resign. I had no idea he was going to do that and I didn't realize Mitch would have to find someone to be blamed. Believe me, Paige, I didn't want Jeff to be the scapegoat."

Yet he hadn't done anything to prevent it. An unexpected fury boiled inside her and for a moment she hated Edward. When the moment passed and the emotion didn't, she knew she had to get away from the claustrophobic confines of the office. She couldn't keep listening. She couldn't bear to continue watching Edward shrink from her distinguished, respectable stepfather into a sick and pathetic old man.

"What about the Tri-Star papers?" Jeff asked. "Didn't you know I'd be the scapegoat there too?"

"You couldn't leave well enough alone. You had to start asking questions about Gary and the contracts his company had picked up in the past two years. I tried to warn you. You just didn't get the message."

"Edward, you—" Jeff's voice broke.

Paige stood and took his hand, sharing his emotion and the sickening taste of disillusionment. "Take me home, Jeff, please." She forced herself to look at her stepfather once more. "We'll discuss the best way to handle your—resignation—later today." Her tongue fought with the necessity of saying the words, but he had left her no choice. She closed her eyes against the threat of tears. "In the meantime, Edward, I think you'd better tell Mother."

His hand stroked his narrow chin in a familiar, nervous gesture. "Mary," he said as if it hadn't occurred to him that she would have to know. But somehow he seemed to find some comfort in the thought of her and his stern composure softened. "I'll do that."

Then as if everything was just as it ought to be, his shoulders straightened and he nodded toward the envelope Paige held. "Do you want me to return that to security?"

"We'll take care of it." Jeff put his hand at Paige's waist and together they turned. As they left the office she thought there should have been something else to say, but she didn't know what.

A soothing numbness cushioned her from facing too much reality all at once. She was able to walk through the building without thinking about the changes about to happen within the company. And she was able to return the Tri-Star spec sheets to security and disarm the rumors of stolen papers with hardly a tremor in her voice. It was Jeff, though, who was actually responsible for her composure. In the complex jumble of her thoughts, she was constantly aware of his presence beside her, of his love surrounding her.

When they reached the privacy of home, he understood her need to be alone. When the anger came, he was there to listen. When the tears came, he offered the comfort of his arms. And when she could, at last, accept the overwhelming sadness, he was there to point out the silver lining.

"I don't understand why you're not angry, Jeff." They were outside, on the back deck. The horror of the day was ending and evening was descending in a cool twilight breeze. Paige sat on the bench swing, one foot tucked beneath her, her hands wrapped around a sweaty ice-filled glass. Jeff stood nearby, leaning against the redwood railing, wrapped up in watching her. "You have every right to be."

"I've been angry, Paige, for almost two years. I think that's long enough."

"But you could—"

"Yes, I could . . . if I was willing to waste my time and emotions on the past. Life is too short for that, Paige. I lost everything once because I had too much pride. I lost you and I misplaced my self-respect for a while, but now I want to put all that behind me. Without you, I was only half the person I wanted to be. Even though finding out that Edward committed the thefts is a sad conclusion to an unhappy story, it *is* a conclusion."

This was a new side to Jeff, a part of him she hadn't known before, and the wonder of discovering him all over again welled inside her. "I don't think I ever realized until now, Jeff, how very special you are. I was so caught up in creating the illusion of a perfect marriage, I forgot all the reasons I fell in love with you in the first place."

"We let the important things get buried in a fog of jealousy and misunderstandings, didn't we?" His lips curved in gentle acceptance.

"And when the NaeComp papers turned up missing, we were too angry and afraid about what was happening to our relationship to handle the strain. I know I shouldn't have made up an alibi for you that day, Jeff, but I didn't know how else to cope with the accusations. I hope you believe I never, not for a single minute, thought you had anything to do with the theft."

"I believe you, Paige, and I know if I'd faced the situation then instead of running from it, you would have stood by me."

"But my love for you wouldn't have been as strong as it is now, Jeff. We've survived crisis and separation. That almost makes all of the pain worthwhile, doesn't it?"

He opened his arms and she walked into them, leaving behind the glass and taking his heart in her empty hands. "I love you, Jefferson Lawrence," she said. "Will you marry me . . . again?"

"When you put it like that, how can I refuse?" He bent his head and brushed her lips with deliciously tender promises. For long, enchanting minutes, Paige lost herself in loving him. When reality intruded, as she supposed it always would, she kept him securely in her arms and accepted the sheltering concern he offered.

"I feel a little guilty, Jeff. With all that's happened

and with everything we still have to face, it seems almost sinful to be so happy." She lifted her eyes to his. "And I am happier than I've been in years."

He smiled and trailed a finger across her cheek. "So am I. We're not going to let the bad times ahead spoil this for us, Paige. We're going to forgive Edward, and as soon as possible we're going to forget the hurt he caused. Things are going to change. He'll have to resign and Mary is going to be upset, but she'll stand by him through this."

Paige hadn't thought much about her mother's reaction, but she knew Jeff was right. Mary cared deeply for Edward Glendenning and she would find forgiveness and understanding. Paige felt a twinge of guilt that in similar circumstances, when Jeff had most needed her support, she had failed him. If Jeff could forgive her that lack of maturity, though, then what right did she have not to forgive herself? She hugged him closer.

"As soon as this is over and things settle down at the company, I'm moving in with you." She felt his surprise in the sudden tensing of his muscles. "Didn't I tell you how much I liked your house? I might even find time to do a little redecorating. But then again, I might not. I hope you won't mind if I go back to college."

He tipped up her chin with his finger. "You're certainly full of plans."

"Any objections?"

"Can't think of a single one. Are you sure, though, you won't mind moving to Oklahoma City?"

"I'll think of it as a long-term honeymoon. Besides, my heart has lived there for a couple of years already."

"Then it's time you came home." He brought his lips to hers in a lingering kiss, and Paige welcomed the beginning of a new life and a second chance at loving. It was almost night and she knew there were some dark days just ahead, but morning would eventually dawn again.

Yes, Paige thought. Come morning, she'd be going home.